Bed

Bed

stories by Tao Lin

MELVILLEHOUSE
BROOKLYN, NEW YORK

© 2007 Tao Lin

Melville House Publishing
145 Plymouth Street
Brooklyn, NY 11201

www.mhpbooks.com

First Melville House Printing: April 2007
    4 5 6 7 8 9 10

Book Design by Kelly Blair

These stories, in slightly different form, appeared as follows:

"Love is a Thing on Sale for More Money Than There Exists" in *Other Voices*; "Three-Day Cruise" in *The Cincinnati Review*; "Suburban Teenage Wasteland Blues" in *The Portland Review*; "Sincerity" in *Dirt Press*; "Love is the Indifferent God of the Religion in which Universe is Church" in *Spork*; "Cull the Steel Heart, Melt the Ice One, Love the Weak Thing; Say Nothing of Consolation, but Irrelevance, Disaster, and Nonexistence; Have No Hope or Hate—Nothing; Ruin Yourself Exclusively, Completely, and Whenever Possible" in *Fourteen Hills*; "Nine, Ten" in *Bullfight Review*; "Insomnia for a Better Tomorrow" in *Opium Magazine*; "Sasquatch" in *The Mississippi Review*.

A catalog record for this book is available from the Library of Congress.

Printed in the U.S.A.

Contents

Love is a Thing on
Sale for More Money
than There Exists

This was the month that people began to suspect that terrorists had infiltrated Middle America, set up underground tunnels in the rural areas, like gophers. During any moment, it was feared, a terrorist might tunnel up into your house and replace your dog with something that resembled your dog but was actually a bomb. This was a new era in terrorism. The terrorists were now quicker, wittier, and more streetwise. They spoke the vernacular, and claimed to be philosophically sound. They would whisper into the wind something mordant and culturally damning about McDonald's, Jesus, and America—and then, if they wanted to, if the situation eschatologically called for it, they would slice your face off with a KFC Spork.

People began to quit their jobs. They saw that their lives were small and threatened, and so they tried to cherish more, to calm down and appreciate things for once. But in the end, bored in their homes, they just became depressed and susceptible to head colds. They filled their apartments with pets, but then neglected to name them. They became nauseated and unbelieving. They did not believe that they themselves were nauseated, but that it was someone else who was nauseated—that it was all, somehow, a trick. A fun joke. "Ha," they thought. Then they went and took a nap. Sometimes, late at night and in Tylenol-cold hazes, crouched and blanket-hooded on their beds, they dared to squint out into their lives, and what they saw was a grass of bad things, miasmic and low to the ground, depraved, scratching, and furry—and squinting back! It was all their pets, and they wanted names. They just wanted to be named!

Life, people learned, was not easy. Life was not cake. Life was not a carrot cake. It was something else. A get-together on Easter Island. You, the botched clone of you, the Miami Dolphins; Coco-Puffs, paper plates, a dwindling supply of clam juice. That was life.

TAO LIN

The economy was up, though, and crime was down. The president brought out graphs on TV, pointed at them. He reminded the people that he was not an evil man, that he, of course, come on now—he just wanted everyone to be happy! In bed, he contemplated the abolition of both anger and unhappiness, the outlawing of them. Could he do that? Did he have the resources? Why hadn't he thought of this before? These days he felt that his thinking was off. Either that, or his thinking about his thinking was off. He began to take pills. Ginseng, Ginkoba. Tic-Tacs. It was an election year, and the future was very uncertain. Leaders all over the globe began to go on TV with graphs, pie charts, and precariously long series of rhetorical questions.

This was also the month that Garret and Kristy stopped experimenting with caffeine. They had, in their year and a half together, tried all the coffees, cut back to tea, tried tea and coffee together—thinking that tea caffeine was different than coffee caffeine—tried snorting tea, swallowing coffee beans, tea cakes, and had then gone back to coffee.

Now they were using caffeine pills. One per day, like a vitamin—tacitly, with only a little shame.

They went to college in Manhattan and lived together in Brooklyn, where the sky was a bleeding-mushroom gray and the pollution seemed to rise directly off the surface of things—cars, buildings, the ground—like a foul heat, a kind of gaseous, urban mirage.

Garret would occasionally glimpse something black and fizzy moving diagonally across the reddening sky. He often suspected that The Future Was Now. Was the future now? Or was it coming up still? He had seen all the apocalypse movies of the 90's, and all the signs were here: the homeless people rising up and walking around, the businessmen entering the parks and sitting down, sitting there all day, leaving late at night—*why?*; the focus on escape—people always talking about escaping to California, Hawaii, Florida; and the stalled technology, how all that was promised—underwater houses, hover cars, domed cities on the moon, robots that would shampoo your hair and assure you that everything was going to be okay—was not here, and would probably never be here. They had lied. Someone had lied.

Garret's dreams were increasingly of normal things that, because of their utter messagelessness, had very natural-seeming undertones of foreboding and impending doom to them. In one dream, Garret was in the shower. He soaped himself, dropped the soap, picked up the soap, put it adjacent the shampoo, and read the shampoo bottle. "Pert Plus," it said.

"I'm thinking about taking a year off," Kristy said. She was graduating a year early due to summer classes and AP credits. "To figure out who I am. I'm not a basketball star. I'm not Jane Goodall. I'm not Mary Stuart Masterson."

It was a Friday morning and they were in bed.

"I always think Jane Goodall is the ape's name," Garret said. "But it's not. It's the name of the blonde lady."

Garret had a psychology lecture today. They decided to meet after, at four, at the deli place.

"The deli with the red thing," Garret said. "Four. Don't be late."

"I'll be there at three-fifty."

"I know you're going to be late," Garret said. Then he left the apartment. Why was Kristy always late? It was winter and raining. The city seemed a place under-siege, an undersea metropolis with a grade-school planetarium dome for a sky, newspapery and cheap, folding down like something soaked. The subway smelled of urine, and some of the streets had long pools of green radioactive sludge on them. Garret went and sat in the deli, which had a red awning. He disliked the word awning. The complete, incomplete word of it. Yawning; they just took the Y off. What was happening? His view was of the sidewalk, a craggy area of Washington Square Park, and some scaffolding. He sat there for a long time, until the deli owner came out from in back to tell him that he couldn't just sit there all day.

Garret nodded and stood. "Sorry," he said.

"Move to Hawaii," said the deli owner. He patted Garret on the back. "Take a jet airplane to Hawaii and be happy."

"Okay," Garret said. He bought a pre-made salad, an orange drink, and a sugar cookie. He thought that he wouldn't go to class. Jesus loves you, he then thought. But Jesus isn't *in love* with you. He thought about that for a while. Awning, he thought. Gnawing. Woodpecker.

Kristy showed up around five. She ran in, her hair wet.

"I forgot you said four," she said. "I was thinking that I was supposed to *leave* at four."

They walked to Union Square, leaning against one another like a weary, wounded people. It was not raining anymore, but the sky was still gray. Kristy asked how Garret's class went. Garret shrugged. They didn't speak anymore after that. They began to sweat, as it was a warm winter. Global warming had finally arrived, maybe. For a long time it was on its way, it was coming, it was imminent, Hollywood made a movie about it, and now it was probably here.

They went in all the stores, then for coffee, and then Garret started making half-hearted jokes about the terrorists. "What if the terrorists opened their own store... and sold bad things?" Garret said. "What would they sell?" he said.

It sometimes seemed to him that for love to work, it had to be fair, that he should tell only half the joke, and she the other half. Otherwise, it would not be love, but something completely else—pity or entertainment, or stand-up comedy. "Well? What they would sell," Garret said. "I can't do everything in this relationship." Sometimes, recently, coffee would make him sleepy and unreasonable and begrudging. He began to remember all the times that Kristy was late, all the times she promised not to be late anymore.

"Yes you can," Kristy said. "You can do anything you want."

"I'm always trying to cheer you up," Garret said. "It seems like this. I'm always trying to make you laugh and you're always depressed."

"What if a terrorist kicked your ass?" Kristy said.

Some areas of the ground had steam coming out of it, and a gigantic truck was coming down the street, like some kind of municipal battering ram. There was always a gigantic truck coming down the street like some kind of municipal battering ram.

"I'm about to do something," Garret said. He bought two rainbow-sprinkled ice cream cones from an ice cream truck, and that was his dinner. "I wanted to, so I did it," he said to Kristy. He looked around to see if anyone was disapproving of this, of two rainbow-sprinkled ice cream cones at once. He almost sneered. Kristy bought a large package of Twizzlers and a coffee the size of a canteen. They went back to Brooklyn, and lay on their bed. Turned off all the lights. And they held each other. "I love you," Kristy said. But she said it softly and Garret didn't hear over the noise of the air conditioner, which bulged out from high on the wall, like a hoary, machine growth, a false but vexing machination—the biscuit-brown plastic appliance *thing* of it, trembling, dripping, clanging, probably not even working.

The radio hit that year was "Sigh (hole)," an R & B song by a pop-rock band:

> There-ere's a hole in you
> Gets emptier, ah-oh, each day
> But you don't needn't be blue
> Everything's-uh gonna be, yeah, okay

For the chorus, the band sighed, caribbeanly, into their microphones. Except the rhythm guitarist, who had to sing-talk, "we are sighing, we are sighing," to let the people know. The music video had celebrities who looked into the camera—looked right at you! *faint!*—and sighed like they really, really, truly meant it. They were sighing at all the distress in the world, people said. Or else because of the ever-invasive paparazzi. There were arguments. Name-calling. People stood up in chain restaurants, pointed diagonally down, and said, "It's because of the paparazzi, you fool." Then they requested a booth table. At night, they sent out mass, illogical, spam e-mails. The celebrities themselves had no comment.

After a psychology lecture, Garret asked a classmate out for lunch. The classmate frowned a little. She had been poking Garret in his shoulder and smiling at him all semester. "Hmm," she said, "I don't think so."

Garret went into the park, where the trees were all leafless. Their petrified-gray branches clawed at the air, like rakes. There was a cemetery wind, dry and slow and slabbed as marble. Elephant graveyard, Garret thought. He sat on a bench and called Kristy. He asked if she wanted to see a movie tonight. She had just gotten out of class, but had another one. "I'll just meet you back at the apartment then," Garret said. He didn't want to see a movie anymore. "I have to study in the library anyway."

"I'll meet you at the library, then," Kristy said.

"I'll just meet you at the apartment. I have to study."

"I won't be late this time," Kristy said. "I'll just meet you at the library."

"No; that isn't it. I just have to study."

"What isn't it?" Kristy said.

"What?"

"Nothing," Kristy said. "Fine then; bye."

Garret went across the street to the library. There was a hole in the sidewalk the size of a bathtub. Construction was being done, was always being done. It was the journey that mattered, Garret thought woozily, the getting-there part. The mayor, and then the president, had begun saying that. "And where are we going?" the mayor had asked. "When will we get there? What will happen to us once we get there?" He really wanted to know.

A woman with a red bandana stepped in front of Garret and gave him a flyer for an anti-war meeting. It was vague to Garret these days what was happening in the rest of the world. He found it difficult to comprehend how large the world was, how many people there were. He would think of the Middle East, of strife and mortar, then suddenly of Australia, and then New Zealand, giant squid, tunafish, and then of Japan, all the millions of people in Japan; and he'd get stuck there, on

Japan—trying to imagine the life of one Japanese person, unable to, conjuring only an image of wasabi, minty and mounded, against a flag-white background.

Garret saw Kristy coming out of a building across the street. He turned, went behind a pillar, and looked. Kristy was with a taller man who had a tiny head. She laughed and the taller man smiled. They went together into another building.

At the anti-war meeting, they wanted to abolish the words "We," "Us," and "Them." Some others wanted to abolish the word "I." They were frustrated. "We this, we that; us this, them that; us vs. them, no wonder things are the way they are." They wanted semantic unity. They were going to make friends with the terrorists. That was their plan. An older man—a professor?—stood and made the case that the terrorists did not want any new friends, had enough friends already, too many, actually; that what they really wanted was romantic love. He was probably a graduate student. Another man stood and said, "Love is a thing on sale for more money than there exists." It seemed an inappropriately capitalist thing to say, or else much too cynical, and the man was ignored. Finally, it was settled: whatever happened, they would just make friends. There were sign up sheets, and then a six-piece jazz-rock band played. The drummer had six cymbals, four of them tiny. People eyed him askance. Was six cymbals, four of them tiny, appropriate for wartime?

Garret walked out into the night, feeling very dry in the mouth, and with a headache. He stood around for a while, and then called Kristy.

"Kristy's at her sister's apartment taking a nap. She's asleep now. I'm her sister."

"You're Kristy's sister?" Garret said.

"Okay. So Kristy's sleeping." She hung up.

One weekend they got out of classes and flew down to Florida, to Garret's mother's house, for a weeklong vacation.

They went to Red Lobster. Kristy ordered the house salad with crabmeat on top.

"I found out I have arthritis in my hands," said Garret's mother. She was taking piano lessons from a young person. Her husband was gone, had found a truer love and was gone, about which she was sometimes jealous, though mostly she felt just sleepy, which she usually interpreted as contentment. She had bought four gas masks, to protect against certain types of terrorism, had wept after she read the instruction manual cover-to-cover, alone, late one night after bathing the dogs.

"Four gas masks," she said. "I feel so stupid. I mean, why four? Why not five, then, or a thousand?" She started to laugh but then stopped and yawned. Kristy looked vertically down at her crabmeat salad. Garret's mother smiled at Kristy's forehead, then asked her son to consider transferring to a school in Florida.

Garret made a noise. He shrugged. He forked at his lobster, which looked mangled and too much like a large insect.

At home, the three of them together tried on the gas masks. They held their faces to the dogs, the two toy poodles, who turned away, went into separate rooms and barked at the walls. They were almost ninety in dog years.

"If I gained thirty pounds," Kristy said in bed, "would you still be with me?"

For love to work, Garret believed, you had to lie all the time, or you had to never lie at all. "I don't know," he said. You had to pick one and then let the other person know which you had picked. You had to be consistent, and sometimes a little stupid. "I can't tell the future," Garret said. "Obviously. Can you?"

A few minutes passed, and then Kristy got up, called the airline place, called a cab, and flew to New York. The next day, though, she flew back, and the rest of the week in Florida was very calm and sunny. They went canoeing, saw fish the size of legs through algae-gauzy water. Garret's mother made a cake. "To Garret and Kristy, with Love: Long and Happy Lives," said the cake. They watched a lot of TV, the three of them on the sofa. Terrorism, polls showed, was now believed to be the largest threat to human safety, ahead of cancer, heart disease, suburban gangs, piranhas, and swimming on a full stomach.

Back in Brooklyn, the new fear was that the terrorists could live inside walls, were maybe already living inside walls—cells of them, entire families, with flashlights, plotting and training, rappelling down the pipes.

Garret began to say things like, "Without coffee I am nothing," and "Terrorism Schmerrorism Berrorrism Schlerorrism," which he said mostly for the torpidity of it, the easy mindlessness of it. He felt that the bones of his jaw and skull were growing, felt the fatty pout of his lips, the discomfort of bigger bones behind his mouth and face. He stopped going to classes, and applied for jobs in Chinatown. He tried not to think. He tried just to love. Anything there was, he tried just to love. It didn't work that way, though. It just didn't. Love, after all, was not sold in bundles, by the pound. Love was not ill-lit, enervated, Chinatown asparagus.

Though if love was an animal, Garret knew, it would probably be the Loch Ness Monster. If it didn't exist, that didn't matter. People made models of it, put it in the water, and took photos. The hoax of it was good enough. The idea of it. Though some people feared it, wished it would just go away, had their lives insured against being eaten alive by it.

Late one night, Kristy got up to use the bathroom.

"What's this on it," Garret said. "Kristy, why are you slamming the door?" He had just had a dream where he walked to a deli and ordered a bagel with cream cheese, but instead received a bagel with something else on it; he couldn't tell what—and then the sound of a door closing.

"I had to use the bathroom," Kristy said.

"Please don't slam the door," Garret said. "Be more considerate." He shifted his head. His hair against the pillow made a loud, prolonged noise—a noise that, before it stopped, seemed as if it might go on forever.

They rarely made love anymore, and only in the mornings, when one of them would wake up, knead against the other, and then start grabbing in that direction. Their heads would be floury and egg-beaten, operating on a kind of toasted, bakery lust, and they'd have sex like that—faces turned away, mouths closed and puffy and hard, eyes scrunched shut.

Afterwards, Garret would feel masturbatory and boneless.

He attended another anti-war meeting. There was another war that was going to happen soon. People stood up and said things. One person said, "People are going to seek happiness. People need to understand that other people are going to do what they think will make them happiest. So people need to just back off, let this happen." She had a ring in her nose, like a bull. The ring was a pale piece of bone. "Revolution is from the inside out," she said. "It's over," someone else said, "the world is done for, doomed—and I say oh well, *oh, well*," then stood and walked briskly out of the room, jumping to slap the top of the doorway on the way out. There was a long moment of nothing, and then a heavy-set, kind-faced man sitting adjacent Garret said loudly, at the ground, "Fuck war, *fuck, war*." People gathered around and patted his back. Some of them, confused and tired, or else just lazy, patted Garret's back, patted anyone's back. There were, again, sign up sheets against the wall. Garret signed up for three different things. He walked out into the city. Drunk people were moving slantly across the sidewalks and streets, though it was only Wednesday.

Garret thought that he might go back to Florida. Maybe get a job on a golf course. He once had a friend who drove one of those armored carts around, vacuuming up golf balls on golf ranges. Maybe he'd do that.

"Come home," Garret's mother said on the phone. "You can take a semester off. Kristy can too. Both of you can come live here and be safe." She said that the terrorists were planning to take hostage the entire island of Manhattan. She had heard on talk radio. They were going to attach outboard motors to Manhattan and drive it like a barge into the Atlantic Ocean. No one knew what the terrorists would do after that, though. Maybe have a cruise around the world, a caller said. Low-key, with virgin pina coladas. Maybe start their own country, another caller said, to legitimize and their terrorism, make it humanitarian and moral and—

He was cut off there.

Kristy had an appointment made to remove her wisdom teeth. She asked Garret to accompany her, but Garret said he had a class that morning. He would meet her after, though.

Kristy's face became lumpy and hard after the operation. "I feel like a monster," she said. They went into an ice cream store, and she began to weep. Garret thought about getting up to hug her, but then just put a hand on her head, across the table. "You look fine," he said. "It won't last, anyway."

Kristy went to her sister's place and Garret went back to Brooklyn.

They didn't talk for a week. Then Garret called her. She said she hadn't called because her face was swollen. She didn't want Garret to see. Garret said he didn't care. They agreed to meet for a movie that night at nine. She said that things would change from now on. She wouldn't be late anymore. They'd go ice-skating.

She came running up for the movie at 8:59. Her face was red and blue on one side; it looked a little bludgeoned, or else diseased.

Garret had the tickets ready and they went in. They watched the trailers and then Kristy reached onto Garret's lap and held his hand. Garret leaned over and whispered, "Come outside a minute, I have to tell you something."

Outside, Kristy smiled at him, and then Garret wasn't sure, but he said it anyway: "If a terrorist said to you that if you were late he'd kill you and your family, would you be one minute early? You wouldn't; you'd be half the fucking day early." He had rehearsed in his head.

"What the hell are you saying, Garret?" said Kristy. "Are you kidding me? Don't do this. You don't know what you're talking about."

But there were things that you had to worry about, Garret knew, that you had to care about. If he didn't say anything, then she would be 20 minutes late, then an hour, then she wouldn't show up at all. Or she'd show up and throw a pie in his face. You had to keep your life under control. Preempt it. You had to let it know that you were not happy. Though maybe you didn't. Maybe it was that you should let things go, be tolerant and easy-going and not ever worry. Ease yourself towards acceptance and quietude, towards, what though—death? No; that didn't seem right. You were supposed to resist death.

"Yeah I do," Garret said. "I'm talking about you shouldn't be late all the time. It's inconsiderate."

"Will you realize what you're saying right now? I was *early* this time."

"I know, but you *ran* here," Garret said. "You could have easily been late."

"So what? I was early."

They stood there for a long time. All the moody emptinesses inside of them swelled and joined, and then ensconced them, like bubbles, and there, inside, they floated—the qualmish, smoked-out bodies of them, stale and still and upside-down. People around them drifted in and out of cars, into stores, across streets and over sidewalks.

"You should have been twenty minutes early," Garret finally said. "You should have thought, 'Hmm, I've been late so many times, maybe I should come much earlier this time, in case one of my excuses comes up to delay me.'"

"You should have been an hour early,"—once he started, he knew, he had to keep going; the anger came from nowhere, it came and was here—"sitting and waiting, to make up for all the hundreds of hours you've been late before, to compensate, to *make sure*." The city lights overlapped in the air, became swimmy, blotchy, and brown. What was reasonable and what was required and what was just plain stupid? Should he apologize? All of life seemed just to be one thing—one slapdash'ed, stuffed turkey of a thing, flying out of the oven and into the night, into orbit; something once familiar and under control, but now just out there, unknown, by itself, charred and brainless and rarely glimpsed.

"That's it," Kristy said. "I'm going to your place right now to get my stuff."

They went back to Garret's apartment. They walked the entire way. Across the avenues and over the Brooklyn bridge. She walked about 20 feet in front. He followed. The night was noisy and black, starless and warm. Maybe it was not winter at all, but summer.

At his apartment, Garret sat on his bed.

Kristy smashed her possessions into her piece of luggage. "You can keep these for your next girlfriend." She held up two mud-green three-pound weights.

"Can you be quiet a little? My suitemate is probably trying to sleep," Garret said. "Why are you so angry, anyway? You're leaving me, so calm down."

Kristy's mouth began to bleed, a slow seeping at the edge, like an early sign of mutation. Her cheek had been swollen for too long. There was maybe something wrong with the stitches. "Fuck," she said. "You didn't even come with me for my wisdom teeth." She wiped her mouth with one of Garret's shirts. "You had to go to class?—you skip all your fucking classes!"

"That's my shirt," Garret said. "That's inconsiderate." Against the bureau was a stack of photos that they had taken together. "Take your photos," Garret said. Kristy kicked them across the floor. She threw her sandals against the wall. They lodged in the window blinds and dust went in the air.

"Why are you acting like this?" Garret said.

Kristy set her luggage upright, the wheels aimed at the door. "Why don't you install soundproof walls for your suitemate?" she said. "If you care about him so much, why don't you?"

"I will," Garret said. "That's considerate of you, finally." They looked at each other. Blood oozed again out of Kristy's mouth, and then out her nose, like a crushed thought. She went and grabbed her sandals from the blinds. She set her luggage outside the door, got in position to properly slam the door with both hands, and then slammed it. The door bounced off its frame without closing.

Kristy wheeled her luggage down the outside hall. It made squeaky noises, and train track noises. Garret sat and listened. For a moment he felt sorry for her, for himself, for the whole wrecked and blighting world—it was hopeless, really—but then he felt okay, felt that things were not that bad; he felt friendly, and he felt that this moment of softness, of calm, though maybe it was just that he was tired, was good, was enough, that if there could be this feeling, then things would go on, month after month, one good and tiny feeling per; it was okay. And he wanted suddenly, badly, to share all this, and so he called out, "Have a good week." He stood and shouted, "Wait; I hope you can be happy now; I hope we can be friends still, really," and then Kristy was back, was looking, was saying, "You're a real shithead," was saying some other things, her face inflamed, and the door, then, slamming shut, making a loud noise.

Three-Day Cruise

After they euthanatize the poodle, they go on the Bahamas cruise. After that, the dad dies of a brain tumor that no one knew about. The mom, then, at Cocoa Beach, teaching herself to swim, drowns; and the son, Paul, too, dies, when he one night sees a car crash happening, is looking, passing by, but then has a dull thought—some sudden vapid mood that almost puts him to sleep—yawns, and swerves, in an abstractly wanting and participatory way, toward the crash. He accelerates, misses, and drives into a pole.

The daughter, Mattie, goes on living. She sometimes shuts her eyes, tight, and then opens them again, placing herself in next week's Sunday. It's a kind of time travel. Something make believe, for kids. Though of course, Mattie knows, she is not a kid. She is in her thirties, in Florida, where she grew up. She has returned. She sometimes feels as if there is a quick-person, five minutes ahead of her, living her life before she gets there. There is one week in all the others when she joins a gym, buys expensive facial creams, and sits sipping broth in the food courts of shopping malls. It is not a bad week. She remembers that week. Then she doesn't remember it. She remembers nothing. All her memories go to noise, go satirical and loud and uncontrollable—they fly like teeth and balloons from her brain to the open bones of her eyes, and clang there, lodge and impact and burst there. The months accumulate like houses in the middle of nowhere. And her sense of irony, finally, her cheap way of paradox, of that self-blanking kind of truth and calm, of easing, sometimes, into the sarcastic haze of living—it goes bad, like an awful, leaden, jam-packed something in her head. Mattie is eating a sandwich. She is scribbling poems on envelopes. She is distracted, she is old. She is dead from something that makes her forget what it is before it kills her.

TAO LIN

Mattie is twelve. She feels, today, for the first time, that happiness is something behind her, something mousy and slick and sliding away, into some hole, into some hole of that some hole.

"Do you ever feel sad?" says Mattie. She and Paul are at the supermarket. She is looking at a blow-dryer box, the woman on which has her hair in such a way that she must, Mattie thinks, be flying.

"What's happier," says Paul. He is six. "The most happy rabbit in the world? A man that is normal happy? A cookie? Between one and a hundred how happy is a cookie? A green one." They are at the supermarket for AAA batteries.

"Forty," says Mattie. "Wait. A green one?" She's looking at the blow-dryer box. "I can't see out my right eye," she says. "It's blurry. Oh, now I can."

"Oh," says Paul. He giggles. "What kind of batteries won't rip you off? This one has Michael Jordan on it. Michael Jordan is funny."

"This lady is flying. This is… unacceptable," says Mattie. She's thinking about dirt—dirt on the ground, in hair, dirt in the sky. She had a dream about dirt. "I hate… school."

"Why?" says Paul. He looks stricken for a moment, a little horrified.

"I'm twelve," says Mattie. "I'm twelve years old!"

"Michael Jordan is strange," says Paul.

They buy Energizer batteries. The parking lot gleams from all the cars. They cross the street, into their neighborhood. Some older kids are gliding around on rollerblades, playing street hockey. One little girl has a baseball bat and is chasing a few of the others. It is sunny and October and breezy. "The air tickles," says Paul. He has Michael Jordan in his head, and can't stop giggling. He blocks the wind from his neck with strangling motions and says, "My hands tickle!" In front of their house, he cartwheels onto grass. He runs at Mattie and jump kicks the air in front of her. Mattie pats his head. Paul goes and hops, circuitously, over a red flower plant. He looks at Mattie and then runs into the house, the front door of which is open.

The mom is in the side yard, watering a palmetto with the hose. Her dress is a bit wet, and her hair too. She waves at Mattie. Their toy poodle is sitting very still on top of the mailbox. He is overheated, but has retained good posture. He looks content in a once-wild way.

Mattie waves at her mom and carries the poodle into the living room.

On the sofa, Mattie pets the poodle until it is dark outside. She lies down. She stares sideways through the sliding glass door, at the sky. In third grade she told some classmates that their teacher, Mrs. Beonard, looked like a dolphin, even though Mrs. Beonard looked very much like an owl. She surprised herself then, and liked it.

Mattie sits up, carries the poodle into her room. She arranges it so they lie facing each other on the bed. The poodle is submissive and inaudible. Mattie closes her eyes, and sees her own face. A nerd, she thinks. Someone at school had called her a nerd. She tries not to think about dirt. Her dream about dirt wasn't a good dream. She sneezes. Her head rings—resonates, like a padded bell. The poodle stands. Mattie pets him until he is flat again. She keeps her hand on his body. She sneezes again, hard, the hardest sneeze she has ever sneezed, and this time there's an exquisite, high-pitched squeak from the pappy center of her head, and then she feels perceptually enhanced—honed and lucid as a tiny, soap-washed moon. She closes her eyes. She hears new things. She hears her own shouldery hipbone, low and curving, sounding purly, cello tones. She hears an ant, in the yard, walking up a blade of grass. She falls asleep and wakes up early in the morning, wide-eyed and alert, four hours before school.

The dad goes around one Saturday with a notepad, taking orders for lunch. He goes out, comes back. "Who ordered the toy poodle?" he says. He's holding, in a manhandled way, an apricot-hued poodle, who is a girl. He points at his notepad. "Says here..."

"I ordered that!" says Paul. He is eight. He is taking all the credit for this, in case of future situations. "I knew to order something good like that." He looks around. The world, he feels, is becoming less, is closing in, trying to detain him, clamp him like a bug. He takes the apricot poodle and runs away.

The mom is going around the house, watering her many potted plants.

Mattie comes out from her room, gets the other poodle, goes back to her room.

In bed, the dad says, "It's fair." He's thinking about the poodles. It's a few years later. "One poodle per child. One male, one female."

"Yes," says the mom. "Fair." She has discovered, going through the trash, envelopes postmarked Nevada, from someone named Scarlet Leysen. The dad had taken a business trip there. Two females per male, the mom thinks. "Life isn't fair," she says. "So we should comport extra fair, to compensate." She used to say, "Life isn't fair, but that doesn't mean we can't try to make it fair," but changed it one day while eating a peach, when she was twenty.

"I know," says the dad. "I agree." He goes to pat the mom's shoulder, but pats the bed instead. He moves his hand through the dark and pats it down again, on the mom's face. Her lips and teeth are wet; she has just licked them. "Sorry," says the dad. He gets up, washes his hands, goes out into the rest of the house.

The mom dreams of the dad, dreams that he descends through a trapdoor, into a room that spins. He crouches, leaps, pushes a button on a wall. A rope ladder appears. He catches it, helicopter-style, climbs it, and is back in the bedroom. He lies down. He rolls over, toward her. His head is snoring and fat and looming, and she is afraid. She wakes up and there he is. His head is snoring, but not fat or looming; he is smiling a little.

In the morning, the mom goes looking for the envelopes. She doesn't find any. She sits down with a microwaved waffle, a bowl of dried cranberries, a canister of whipped cream. She plays back the dream in her head. She likes the rope ladder part. She holds the whipped cream vertically down, as it says to on the canister.

Over time, the mom makes herself forget the envelopes, which works, until one day, going through mail, she finds that she has been looking for a very long time at this letter from Nevada with Smurf stickers all over it—Smurfs dressed in pink, Smurfs smooching. She throws a pencil and a wristwatch into the swimming pool. She frowns and paces. She throws a muffin on the floor and doesn't clean it up. This is her little rampage. She locks herself in her bedroom and sits very still on her bed. The world sits beside her, the size and intelligence and badness of a cupcake. In her head, there is a steady, clear-voiced scream, pitched in middle C. It is not unpleasing. She listens to it for some time and then lies down.

The dad is made to sleep on the couch. He buys his own blanket from Kmart, a green one, and a pillow that is supposed to be for dogs. He sleeps with a box of sugar cookies on his chest—something, he knows, that he has always wanted. Instead of toothbrushing, he has mints.

The mom misses the dad. She does not speculate on Scarlet Leysen. She destroys Nevada out of her head, the entire state. She makes it have a lava-y Earthquake. She mostly forgives the dad. Still, though, she knows, the dad should be punished. She begins to make dinner only for herself, Paul, and Mattie. She tries not to look at the dad when they are in the kitchen together. Once, though, she glances and sees that the dad's mouth is moving and that he is lining up three uncut pickles on a piece of bread. They make eye contact and his mouth keeps moving, noiselessly, and then he loudly says, "—and I'm competent." The mom looks away. She grins. She leaves the kitchen. She is a little giddy. Control yourself, she thinks. Each day of punishment is a delay of gratification, an investment towards better, future love.

"Tell your mom to stop being angry at me," says the dad one night to Paul. He is at the fax machine, on a stool, has his head turned around to Paul, who is on the sofa watching TV.

"You," says Paul. He is eleven. He has changed. He is somewhat fat, and his head has grown, he thinks, too big. Some nights, in bed, he spreads his fingers evenly over his skull and pushes inward and counts to one hundred. He has to do something, he knows, contain it—not unlike braces for teeth, which he has. Sometimes he looks in the mirror and imagines a team of dwarves, swarming, smacking at his body. Once, he dreams this. "Hey now," he says in his dream. There is a doorway and the dwarves keep rushing in. "Hey," he says. "Why?"

"She listens to you; not me," says the dad. He moves his face close to Paul's. It is a bewildered, distracted face—the face of someone clearly without secrets, but still somehow untrustable. "She doesn't listen to me," he says. He has just invented a new laser, that afternoon. "You need to tell her. Say to her—"

The fax machine begins to make noises and the dad attends to it.

"You," says Paul. He bites in half his cream-filled Popsicle. He makes a face. His favorite thing to do, now, is to eat something concocted and sludgy—cherry pie-chocolate syrup pudding, marshmallow-maraschino cherry soup—and then, sweet and sticky mouthed, lie down for a nap. He likes to be sleepy, likes the keen apathy and warm coolness of it.

After a few weeks the dad is allowed back in the bedroom.

He is smiling and clear-eyed. "That was terrible," he says. "You were so angry. I tried to impress you by eating healthy." He chuckles. "You were so angry!" He smiles and moves to her and hugs her.

Weekends, the dad puts on swimming trunks, swims two or three laps, then gets distracted and goes, dripping, into the house, to find the poodles. He enforces direction and speed as the poodles are made to swim repeatedly from the deep end to the shallow end. He mock screams at them. The mom has the camcorder. She encourages Paul and Mattie to swim. After the poodles, the dad spends time—too much time, everyone agrees—with the long-handled scrubber, scrubbing at all the fey and faint patches of pool algae.

For dinner the dad is made to eat a bowl of steamed vegetables. He has high cholesterol and is not allowed to eat shrimp or egg yolk. He sometimes complains, but is generally docile and obedient. "Poodles are natural water dogs," he says. "In France, they live in the rivers. Caves of them. Lined up and ready. They ascend one by one. They bob skyward, like penguins. They paddle carefully, heads up, barking at a polite and tactful volume and timbre. People toss them food." The dad chuckles. He has amused himself. "A river crammed with poodles," he says. "Imagine that. Have salmon, then have poodles instead of salmon." He falls asleep on the carpet by the television. He sleeps with his mouth open. His teeth are crooked in a lightly shuffled way and smell of hot summer weeds.

Christmas, the mom has her camcorder. The poodles have their own presents. Neon flea collars, a rubber cheeseburger, a rubber foot! The Christmas tree is plastic and has, mysteriously, over the years, turned from a dark green to a bright and fiery orange. The dad is sheepish and aloof. He has never bought anyone a present. It is just something that he doesn't do; something about his childhood. He doesn't seem to understand. He is an inventor. He leaves the room for a moment. He comes back carrying a big gift-wrapped thing. He sets it on the ground. "Hurry," he says. "Who's it for?" says Paul. "You," says the dad. Paul opens it. It is their two toy poodles. The poodles look around, then move carefully away. The dad almost falls to the carpet. He laughs a kind of laugh that none of them have heard before.

Mattie goes to college in New York City, where she takes too many creative writing courses.

She dislikes enjambment, symbolism, the Best American Poetry series. She writes indignantly, with a kind of whirlpooling impatience. Though sometimes she imagines that her hair is white and fluffy, and then she writes cutely, with many l's, as if to a future grand-daughter of hers—some mute and dreamy girl, in a future, enchantless world, without trees or sidewalks.

In Mattie's head, she critiques other people's critiques of her work.

"I have no idea what I'm doing here," she says to classmates. "In college, I mean. Do you?"—here, she likes to lean in close—"Do you know?" One night, she steps off the curb into the street. There is a breeze and her hair sweeps across her face. The street is calm and quiet; there seem to be no other people around. She closes her eyes. A bus that is two buses, swingy and accordioned, comes at her. The bus does not honk. She very slowly opens and closes her eyes, and then crosses the street. She sometimes wonders if she died that night. She remembers the wind, the lightless blacktop, the phantom bus that does not honk.

After college, Mattie stays in New York.

Paul is now in Boston, for his own college education. "I used to walk home to my apartment thinking about crying," he writes in email to Mattie—the mom has encouraged her children to email one another—"three in the morning. Carrying bags of groceries. Finally, I'd cry a little. It was a long walk. I'd put everything into the refrigerator including the plastic bags and go to sleep. In the morning, I'd eat four bowls of Frosted Flakes, go back to sleep. But that gradually stopped. That time of my life. Today, I am changed. Tolerance, life, it moves you to the center of things. How have you been?"

"Then it kills you," writes back Mattie. She likes Paul. They get each other. They do. "It moves you, then it kills you. It says, 'Move here,' then kills you. It puts its hands on your shoulders, moves you, kills you."

Once, they see each other. In Barnes and Noble by Union Square. Mattie sees Paul first, a passing glimpse, the recognition coming a few seconds later. She becomes confused—Paul should be in Boston—and, for a long while after, does not trust herself, feels vaguely that she has suffered some kind of cosmic accident. Is she in

Boston? What does that mean? To be in Boston? Later, Paul sees Mattie as she is going down the escalator and he is going up. They seem to look each other in the face. Mattie has an abstract expression, and Paul thinks of screaming her name, but then thinks that that would be a bit ridiculous. Later, he thinks of just saying her name, at a normal volume. Of course, he thinks. They don't ever mention this to each other and, over time, begin to doubt that it happened.

The dad is one day accused by the government of having released false and misleading press releases. It has to do with the company he has founded for his inventions.

In the courtroom, the jury is working-class, weary, and stadium seated—to one side, like one of those multiple missile launchers. The dad's lawyer has not had a good childhood, and now, in adulthood, is often depressed, shy, and nervous—nevertheless the dad trusts him.

The government lawyer is daunting and loud.

In low-security federal prison camp, the dad is productive and healthy. He makes many friends. The inmates are sanguine and witty; ninety-percent are in for drugs. They debate, cook, play poker and ping-pong, watch TV, work out, plan future criminal activity, make criminal connections, study law.

The dad is to be there for seventy months.

The mom visits twice a week. It is a two-hour drive. "Did you feed the dogs?" says the dad. "Dogs are people too."

They talk on the phone. "Don't tattle," says the mom. She has written down a list of things that the dad should not do. "Don't complain, don't spread rumors." She goes to sleep very early now. Her dreams undergo change. They begin to occur nightly—fully formed, with beginnings, middles, and ends. They have subtle plotting and good dialogue.

In the daytime, the mom walks around the house with a new excitement. In emails to her children, she expresses amazement at her own brain. She feels a bit powerful. "I dream every night," she writes, "how about you?" In one dream, the family goes on a Bahamas cruise, has a great time. The mom swims in the dream, though she cannot swim in real life. At dinner in the dream, the mom glances across the hall, notices a girl who has very small teeth, goes over there, asks the girl to open her mouth, and wow! The girl has many layers of teeth—thousands! The mom tells her so, and everyone laughs.

In the morning, the mom looks into and buys four cruise tickets, for when the dad is released from prison.

She and the dogs, walking around the house, sometimes cross paths. They look at one another, make sure not to collide, and continue on to where they are going. Though sometimes the mom blocks the dogs, shunts them into corners—or follows them, at a distance. Mostly, the mom finds, the dogs just walk from one room to another, where they then lie down, sphinx style—a style they have recently taken to for some reason.

Summer nights, when it is black and hot and humid outside, the mom gets a little confused. She gets a panicked feeling that the dad, Mattie, and Paul have all, a long time ago, run off with Scarlet Leysen. She forgets the names of the days of the week. She feels ageless and illusory. She is afraid that she will wake one night and find that her pillow is a dismembered torso, that she has murdered a person! She fears the poodles, that there are two against her one, fears the team of them, the ready conspiracy of them. One night, she hears noises. She turns on all the lights, moves quickly to the sofa, lies on her side, turns the TV to the Weather Channel—the least scary channel, she knows—and thinks hard about Mattie, Paul, and the dad, gets them all talking in her head, then calls softly for the poodles.

In prison, the dad has obtained three patents, published eight papers—through collaboration with the mom—and begun to read Chuang Zhu, other Eastern Philosophers, and books on death. He writes to Mattie and Paul. "I am doing an aerobics class two times a week. I am in charge of a team of people. We dig up grass, plant grass, do things with grass. My daily routine is—" and it says his daily routine.

The mom text messages Mattie, "Just saw a reporter blown away by wind on TV." She emails Paul, "This morning I yelled 'scumbag' and the dogs came running from their rooms with eyes so big, anticipating, they must think scumbag is something delicious."

The apricot poodle is found to have diabetes. The mom is to inject her with insulin twice daily, which goes okay for a while, until one morning, when the apricot poodle is dead. The mom has been injecting her with air instead of insulin. She buries the dead poodle in the backyard. She carries around the other poodle—who can barely see anymore and sometimes walks into walls—the rest of that day and forgets to feed him.

The prison doctor one day says that the dad's kidney is engorged, but it turns out to be nothing.

For a year, no one hears from Paul. Then they hear from Paul. He claims to have lived in Canada for some time. He has read a book called "Into The Wild," in which a boy graduates college, donates his money to OXFAM, wanders the country alone, hitchhikes into Alaska, writes in his journal that happiness is only real when shared, and, wrapped in a sleeping bag, then, inside an abandoned bus, nearby a frozen river, dies. It's a non-fiction book and Paul recommends it.

The dad is released.

The remaining poodle has begun to twitch. He has cataracts and his gums bleed. He stops eating. Mattie flies home. They broil a pork chop and set it in front of the poodle. The pork chop smells good. It is hot at first but quickly turns cold. The poodle looks at it but does not move.

They all, except Paul, whose plane is delayed, bring the poodle to the pet hospital and have it put to sleep.

Paul arrives in the night, by taxi. He has gained more weight. He looks generally less effective, as a person. He has a friend with him, Christine, who looks worried, and keeps touching her hair.

The cruise is underbooked and overstaffed. It has the casually terminal feel of a nice retirement home—something of zoo-animal complacency and over-the-counter drug proliferation. The railings and walls are clean and shiny, but in an enforced and afflicted way that seems a little sarcastic.

Still, the food is excellent and the passengers are all very happy.

The staff is inspiriting and Filipino.

At dinner, Christine sits alone at a table on the other side of the dining room. She insists on this, says because she isn't part of the family. She eats slowly and carefully—in open view of the family's table—with her face down, and worried. No one seems to know how or when she bought a ticket.

The next day, there is a lunch buffet on the sun deck.

"Let's take five minutes before we eat to think about death," says the dad. They are seated adjacent the pool, which is covered, for now, with a gleaming white tarp. "What it is. How to defeat it. Strategies, options. What are we dealing with? After, we'll share."

The mom likes this about the dad. As a child, she'd always had what she imagined were fascinating thoughts, but didn't ever say them. Once, as a little girl, at recess, she thought that if she ran very fast at a pole and then caught it and swung quickly around, part of her would keep going, and she would become two girls. That same day, sitting on the monkeybars, she also had an idea for a movie—a mystery/horror movie. Someone would wake one morning and find that their pillow had been replaced with a dismembered torso!

"Okay," says the dad. He points at Christine. "You first."

"Death is a toad," Christine says loudly. She makes a defeated face. "A toad... in outer space. It has a cape." She opens her mouth. She seems stunned. "Besides the cape, it's a normal toad."

The dad looks at the mom.

"Death is the end of the dream," says the mom. She blinks. She enunciates carefully. "When you wake up finally, you find that there was nothing real after all." She brings her fruit punch to her mouth, looks down into it, and sips.

"Death is the plural of deaf," says Paul. "It's when everything goes deaf."

"Oh," says Christine. She stands up, sits back down.

"Death is an emotion outside all the other emotions," Mattie says, looking at Christine, who has a worried expression on her face. "A comet, blackblue, fast as ice." She is quoting one of her poems. The next line is a non-sequitur, *the men look two inches into my forehead*, as are the next couple of lines, *i ask for no receipt / but am given a receipt / forced to take it home / unfurl it / like a scroll / staple a wall to it*. There are more lines, a rant on the bronze dirtiness of pennies. It is a long poem. Mattie skips to the end. "Death is a highly polished thought." She feels dazed and shy and occult.

"Is that one of your poems?" says the mom. She smiles.

Mattie nods carefully. There were more lines, actually, she now remembers, *life is the sarcastic joke of death / and death is the sarcastic mouth that eats the ironic food / the organic water / the life that fills with teeth / the pecans you like, the nuts / the hardened brains of smaller animals*. It just kept going, that poem.

"Death is the end of the fear of death," says the dad. "To avoid it we must not stop fearing it and so life is fear. Death is time because time allows us to move toward death which we fear at all times when alive. We move around and that is fear. Movement through space requires time. Without death there is no movement through space and no life and no fear. To be aware of death is to be alive is to fear is to move around in space and time toward death."

They arrive at port in the Bahamas. There are five other gigantic cruise ships. There is the sun-toned city of Nassau, with its conch divers, horse-drawn carriages, cool-black men and women—all in view, yards away—but the tourists are funneled onto a ferry and taken to some other island, where there is a buffet, a pavilion, a long, pragmatic beach, and an inner-tube hut.

They sit facing the ocean. Christine sits straight-backed on the edge of a lounge chair. Mattie lies on an adjacent lounge chair. Paul and the dad are on the pier—there is a low, kid-sized pier—observing some fish. The mom is standing back, on a grassy area, drinking a tropical drink. She is thinking about in her dream, when she was swimming. It was here. Was it here?

"Why are you worried?" Mattie asks Christine. "You seem worried, I mean."

"I'm…" Christine touches the back of her hand. "The sky… it begins immediately off of our skin. It goes forever, past the stars. Anything beyond can reach down, grab us, pull us off the planet."

"You're just improvising, aren't you?" says Mattie. "When you talk. Each moment, you're just making up stuff. I mean, that's what we all do, I guess. I'm not critiquing." She looks at Christine. A lot of time seems to pass. "It's okay, It's good, I like what you say; the toad thing. I'm not attacking. No; not at all."

Christine stands abruptly up. Her chair makes a noise. She falls to the sand and stands back up. "I'm…" she says. She points wanly in some direction, then goes there, touching her hair and pointing.

That night, they are taken to a hotel that is also a casino and a fish aquarium. There is one wall that is a fish tank of only piranhas. They are the color of mangoes and have flat, koala noses. They all face in one direction, and are all very still, except for a few up top that tremble and look a bit anxious.

"Where's Christine?" asks the mom. Paul shrugs. No

one seems to know. They don't dwell on it. They play roulette. Paul later says, "Christine told me, she said, 'I'm not sure, but I might be disappearing into the islands of the Bahamas.' If anyone's wondering about that."

They sleep on their backs. The ship leaves the Bahamas in the night.

The third day is a day at sea.

At dinner, the dad and the mom sit facing Mattie and Paul.

The mom looks over at Christine's table. A different woman is there. Older, with chandelier earrings, a lot of make-up. Her glass of water is empty and on the edge of her table.

Mattie reads the menu in her head, "...a bed of carrots, broccoli, and four other green," then out loud, "red, healthy, steamed vegetables." She looks up.

"You're the sarcastic one," says the dad. He's looking at Mattie. He brings his hand up from under the table. He points at Paul. "You. What are you? You're sarcastic too, aren't you?"

"I'm the outwardly depressed, inwardly content one," says Paul.

"He's the sarcastic-sarcastic one," says Mattie. "Two sarcastics." She flips her menu over, looks at the back of it.

"I'm the outwardly depressed, inwardly content

one," says Paul.

The soup is green and good. The salad is crunchy, with water droplets all over and in it. Mattie has ordered the steamed vegetables. She eats most of it. She crushes a carrot by pressing down hard with her spoon, which then squeals against the plate. I'm the stupid one, she thinks. She grins a little. She reaches for the sugar, changes her mind, moves her hand to her water, changes her mind, brings her hand to her head, scratches behind her ear.

"I saw that," says the dad. "I saw starting with the childlike behavior with the carrot." He looks at Mattie, at Paul. I made you two, he thinks. He stands and reaches across the table and pats Mattie on the head. He pats Paul, too, on the head. He sits back down. He pats the mom on the head. The mom pats the dad on the head. She smiles. She turns and looks quickly over at Christine's table again.

"Sorry," she says. "I don't know why I keep looking."

That night, after the farewell show in the Moonbeam lounge—a dancing, singing, juggling thing—there is the midnight buffet. It has three ice sculptures. A swan, a bear, a dolphin. The foods are also sculpted. There are owly apples, starfishy cheeses, cookies shaped esoterically like ocean sunfish. People take photos of their plates. They eat cautiously at first, then, having realized something, violently, biting off heads and fins and limbs, grinning. The mom runs down to their room and comes back with the camcorder.

After the buffet, they go up to the top deck. The air is cool, and the ocean, all around, is black and smooth. The stars are rich and streaky, as if behind water. They go down one deck, into a glass-enclosed area. It is late and there are just a few other people here.

There is a ping-pong table. The dad challenges Mattie and Paul. The mom starts up her camcorder, which is digital. "If I lose," says the dad, "I'll buy you both cars." The mom zooms wildly in on the dad's face. She pans back and steps in closer. Paul's body is languid and cascaded, chin to chest to stomach, but his arms are speedy and graceful. The dad stands rigidly, up close to the table. He does not bend his back or twist his hips. He tosses his paddle from hand to hand. "Ambidextrous," he says. He is winning. From his time in prison, he has become an expert at ping-pong. He flips over his paddle and serves with the handle end—a slow, high lob to Paul. Mattie chops the ball down massively, tennis-style, and, while doing that, knocks Paul to the floor. The ball bounces hard and loud and high. The dad leaps and tosses his paddle into the air. The paddle does not connect with the ball. The dad catches his paddle. "Mattie," he says. "Mattie!" The mom's hand is shaking a little. She tries to keep the camcorder steady with both hands. She hears Mattie laughing and Paul saying, "What the hell was that? What was that!" She tries to zoom in on Mattie laughing. She pans back and sees Paul on the floor still. His face is startled and young. He has taken off a shoe. He throws it at Mattie. Mattie whacks the shoe at the dad, who pivots and whacks the shoe behind him, where it goes spinning over the railing into the dark. The mom pushes the camcorder at Mattie's chest. Mattie is laughing and she looks and takes the camcorder. The mom runs off, into the fore of the ship—a dark, open area with lounge chairs, railing, the sky, the ocean. Mattie sets the camcorder down on the ping-pong table. She runs and follows her mom. There is a cool breeze and it is very calm and quiet. The floor is wood. The mom is at the railing. Her form is small and vague.

Mattie goes closer, hears that her mom is weeping, and hesitates. She stops smiling and feels that her cheeks are tired. She glances away, turning her ear flat to the sandpapery roar of the wind, then looks back, quiet again. The mom has turned a little. Mattie has a sudden bad thought and is about to say, "Mom, wait," but the mom now turns fully around. She is crying loud and wet. She steps slowly toward Mattie. She cries with her arms at her sides. "Mattie," she says. She flings a fist up to her shoulder, pushes it back down to her side. There's a contrary draft of wind and the mom's hair sweeps, diagonal, across her face. The ocean behind her is pooling and dark and quietly moving. The sky is black and close. "Oh, Mattie," she says. Her voice is loud and clear. "I'm so happy."

Suburban Teenage
Wasteland Blues

That kind of gnawing *offness* that Greg always felt, that constant knowledge that he was doomed in small but myriad ways, intensified in the presence of people, became immediate and insufferable, like a rat in the stomach. So after his parents sold the house and retired to California, Greg moved alone into an apartment behind a rundown 24-hour supermarket. There he drank coffee, and watched The History Channel. His meals became larger and less often, like a crocodile's. He'd eat an entire package of bacon or a box of frosty muffins, sleep for 20 hours, and then masturbate, languishingly, to all his crushes from middle and high school. He became nocturnal and strange, taking on all the impatience and bipolarity of a young child, without any of the charm or smooth complexion. Sometimes he'd catch himself speaking, in his head, to objects—a thing of food, a box of Kleenex, a door—hesitate, but then continue, keep on going with what he needed to say, finish it off, out loud, because what did it matter, either way?

But then his parents changed. A year of California had changed them. They stopped sending money. Greg was forced to go out into the world, to interact with real people. And he was glad of this. He had always wanted to be a normal person. To be at ease in society. He had just been too scared to try. But now he was forced to, and so he did—he went and got a job at the public library. He was not quite a librarian, but close. Greg was a shelver. There would be carts of books to shelve, then there would be no more carts of books to shelve, then there would be carts of books to shelve.

As a shelver, Greg felt that life was passing him by in a slow and distant, but massive, way—like the moon. Whereas before, reclused in his apartment, Greg felt as if *on* the moon, negotiating all its post-apocalyptic, spaceman barrenness and sometimes eyeing the Earth out there—that gaudy ornament in space—at first with envy, but then with a latent, inaccurate sort of hatred.

It was probably best not to think about your life, though—ever—Greg knew, but to just assume that it was there, and happening, to trust that it was out there, doing whatever it was that a life would do. It was probably best, instead, to spend your time wiping the bathroom floor with wet toilet paper; filling the refrigerator with food, noting the day-to-day depletion of it; looking at stuff and going "Hmm" without thinking anything. Things like that. Things that were neutral and lucid and made profound sense as long as you kept them to yourself, in a secret box concealed from the rest of your brain—a box you then crawled into, like a hiding spot. An end-place.

Still, Greg would think about his life. All the time he would. He'd try to define it. It was a moon. But it was a life, too. It was a thing beyond the moon, if the moon was a hole in the sky. Or it was a cow, a fish. A dodo-bird. He was prone to crude, animal metaphors of life. He would see all of life—the entire askance crash of it, in the side yard, like a UFO—in an ant, a toad. He was prone to metaphors within metaphors. Two metaphors at once. Dashed, and simile'd. He would declare things, try things out: "Life is an ant—so small you just want to smoosh it, that you can't help but smoosh it, that you leave the bathroom telling yourself

you won't smoosh it, but then go back, smoosh it."
Was this right? Did it make sense? He would say these
things out loud, in another person's voice, in the empty
classroom of his head. Often, in a girl's voice. It kept
him company, and passed the time. But it also frightened him; these precarious beginnings of imaginary
friends—was this…safe? It was iffy, Greg knew. Iffy at
best. He was much too old for imaginary friends. He
was 23. He should be in some army infantry unit somewhere—taking off his helmet, wiping his brow, putting
his helmet back on. Or else in grad school, on a futon,
patting a girlfriend's head with one hand and marking
up a textbook with the other. There were infinite other
places where he should be instead of where he was right
now. And this didn't seem right—one over infinity; did-
n't this equal zero? As it turned out—Greg Googled it—
no, it didn't. One in infinity only *tended* towards zero.
But still, it didn't make any sense. How could one trust
the internet?

Greg signed his timesheet and went to the children's
books section. Rachel was sitting Indian style on the carpet. She was new here—another high schooler here for
community service, which helped, supposedly, for college admissions.

TAO LIN

Rachel looked up. "Hey Greg."

"Hi, Rachel." Greg had recently begun calling peo-ple by their names. It had always seemed strange to him—the sudden possession and clinical, Greg felt, inti-macy of it—but now he had started doing it. His co-workers had begun talking. They would tilt their heads, peer into Greg's face like a zoo animal, and then ask him why he was being anti-social. And so Greg had made the effort to speak more. He bought books on how to improve his social skills. One book said to address people by their names. It would be interpreted as friendly. And though his voice still sounded small and weepy to him, like gerbils let into a swamp, Greg felt good to be saying people's names. To be making some kind of progress.

"What's with hippos and kids?" Rachel said. "All these kid's books involve hippos. Either hippos or grapes. What's with that?"

"Where do hippos come from, anyway?" Greg said. "I mean, what are they related to? Elephants? It feels like they're from outer space." Greg could sometimes talk like this. Something inside of him would prop up, and in that quick and windowed moment, something flurried and alive would glide out, and play a little. Then it would fly right back in, though—dead now, and wooden—and knock against Greg's insides, lodging there like a boomerang.

"Outer space?" Rachel smiled. "Dugongs?"

Greg liked Rachel. He would talk to her more. He would say something insightful and ahead of its time—something that should not have been said until 20, 30 years from now. Rachel would beam, then swoon a little. They'd get married. Open a little iced coffee place on the beach, right out of the sand, like a trapdoor. But now Greg's face turned red, which would happen; whenever it wanted, Greg's heart would move up into his face and linger there—hot, throbbing, and bored, like a ten year old.

Rachel watched this, then looked down. There were children's books scattered around her, hard and plate-y, and she began to sort them. "They should do a children's book on dugongs and manatees," she said. "There would be prejudice between them. But in the end they would unite against the sharks."

"Good luck with that," Greg said. "Rachel." It didn't make any sense, and Greg didn't know how he came to say it. But he had mumbled it, anyway, and so Rachel didn't hear. She looked up and smiled. Greg tried to do something with his face—tried to smile back, look happy or something, confident and *grown-up*; like he wasn't afraid of people—but it didn't happen and he turned and moved driftily away, feeling dilute and sick, like watercolors, like a ghost with a cold.

On his lunch break, Greg walked out into the parking lot. He had planned to drive to Wendy's for a Spicy Chicken Sandwich, but Rachel was out here with three friends, all of them leaned up against a truck.

"Greg," Rachel called out. She waved him over.

Greg stumbled a bit, almost fell over. He had forgotten how to walk. Life was precarious like this. You could forget things. You could even float away, Greg knew, like a balloon. Or else topple like a tree, slow-motion and deadpan, teeth smashing into the blacktop. That could happen.

"Hi, Rachel," Greg said. He tried to grin, but his face took on a grieved expression instead. He had no control over such things—his face, anything. Control was illusion. Control was kiddy glue, non-toxic and blue. Though the truth, really, if you wanted it, was that there was no glue, not even kiddy glue. That was a lie. There was nothing holding anything together. Your face could do things you didn't want it to do, and you could say things you never wanted to say. And these sort-of accidents could covey out into the rest of your life, like pigeons, so that when you got there, to the rest of your life, you'd find only—pigeons. You wouldn't know what to do. They'd be making those intrinsic pigeon noises, and you just would not know what to do. Eventually, though, you'd adapt—you'd take to emulating them, mockingly at first, but then earnestly, trying hard to get it right.

Rachel started introducing Greg to her friends. There were five now. Some had come out of the truck. They were talking, but Greg couldn't comprehend anything. He was worrying that his nervousness was showing, trying to control this, worrying that he couldn't.

"Come with us, Greg," said one of them.

Greg felt a need to smile, so he did, but then stopped—it didn't feel right. His face was saying things. It was saying, "I hate you. Go away. Shut up and go home. I hate me. Go home me." It was out of control in a robot way, speaking with a kind of death knell, cheerleader-y rhythm, like something powered on AAA batteries. Something you fixed by hitting it.

"We're going bowling," Rachel said. "Tomorrow night. Come with us."

Greg had an image of someone bowling a strike, then breakdancing—slow at first, but then faster, and then like crazy, breakdancing out of the bowling alley and into the parking lot. But was this how you went about *getting a life*? You went bowling, some other things happened, and then, finally, you were awarded a life? Greg had to try. "Okay," he said. He nodded a few times. People were always talking about *getting a life*, as if there were a store and it was just a matter of going there, picking one out. It annoyed Greg. Though in his sleepier moments, he believed in this store, understood that it was in Europe somewhere, or else deep in Russia. One of those two places. He'd sometimes wake up sad because the store was so far away. Why did it have to be so far away?

"Greg, hey," Rachel said. She did a little hop-step forward, touched Greg's shoulder, sprung back, and giggled a bit. Greg looked down, aware of Rachel's friends, that they were watching him, thinking strange and unknowable things. He scratched the back of his neck, kicked at a patch of pebbles, glanced back up at Rachel. She was smiling and had her eyebrows raised in such a patient and accommodating way that Greg felt, briefly, until he became aware of it, essential, unafraid, and at ease in the world—almost, he thought later, while shelving books, euphoric.

After work Greg stopped at Wendy's. He did the drive-thru, sat in his car in the parking lot. He had the windows down and the air-conditioner on. The steering wheel was warm against his forearms. It felt good. He had a Spicy Chicken Sandwich. He also had a Dr.

Pepper with ice in it. Everything was okay, Greg thought. Everything was fine. He squished some mayonnaise onto his sandwich. Forty or fifty years would pass and then it would be over; maybe something nice would happen in those fifty years, but if not, that was okay. Just sitting here in his car, eating, this was enough. Things weren't that bad. The Spicy Chicken Sandwich tasted good, and it would always taste good. He would talk to Rachel every once in a while. Be friendly with her. That would be nice. With her 75 hours of community service, then, she would go off to college. New girls would come for their own community service. They too would go to college. They'd meet their boyfriends. Marry and live their lives.

Greg began to feel that things weren't okay. A numbed sort of restlessness started in his chest, a lame and disfigured yearning, some mangled need to do something drastic, to get out of himself—to change; but how, and to what? Greg didn't know. He finished his sandwich and drove home, the sun glaring blade-y and white through the windshield. He watched some TV, took extra-strength nighttime Tylenol cold, and lay on his bed. He tried to sleep, then began thinking about an uncle of his. Uncle Larry. At family gatherings, Uncle Larry would always stand to the side, at an oblique.

Sometimes he'd say something and in saying it he'd start looking away, and by the time he was finished saying his little thing—an amusing observation, usually—he'd be looking almost vertically down at the ground. He would very rarely laugh, but when he did, his face would look so kind and meek and sentimental—all crinkled and papery—that Greg, watching, would get an overwhelming urge to go somewhere alone to cry. Usually, though, Uncle Larry's expression would be one of bewildered disappointment—a kind of continual, half-hearted acceptance that things had gone wrong. It was a face that said, "Fuck the world," but said it reluctantly, and tonelessly, and then apologized, said "Sorry," but said all of this so shyly that no one heard, anyway, except for himself. A year ago, Uncle Larry went to the hospital with the flu, somehow fell into a coma, and, a few days later, died. Greg thought about this and wept, and went to sleep.

The next evening, Greg drove to the bowling alley and sat in his car. He was thinking about how to stop himself from worrying when he thought suddenly and lucidly that if he were seven years old he would now—proportionately, or whatever—be hanging out with one-year-olds. A seven-year-old going bowling with babies!

Rachel knocked on his window and he put it down.

"Hey, new plans," she said. "We're going to roll this kid's house. No more bowling. Want to come?"

Greg's heart leapt a bit, left a balloonish impression in his throat. He had done some rolling in high school—unfurling toilet paper in people's yards, in their trees and bushes. It was fun. Except once when his own house had been rolled, it was embarrassing. It was bad. He tried to clean it before his mother saw, but then she came outside and saw. She didn't say anything; just went back inside. Then the neighbor came over, angry—some toilet paper had blown into his yard.

"Who's going?" Greg said.

"Steve, Dan, Liz, everyone." Rachel was smiling. She leaned her forearms on Greg's door, moved half her head inside the car, and started messing around with the levers for the windshield wipers. She smelled good. Greg noticed that from up close her face was very pretty. It startled him a little. He leaned back into his seat and became conscious of his own head, the watermelon-y heave of it.

"So you want to go?" Rachel said. "You do. You drive and I'll ride with you." She pulled on a lever and water squirted out onto the windshield. Her head was now entirely in the car. Greg thought of grabbing it and kissing it, clutching it like a football and taking it home, sleeping nightly with the looted person of it, like some kind of illegal but straightforward substitute for companionship.

"Okay," Greg said.

Rachel went around the front of the car and opened the passenger door, got in. "We're meeting at Wal-Mart," she said. "You know where Wal-Mart is?" She started turning knobs, pressing things. The glove compartment popped open and a map fell out.

At Wal-Mart, Rachel's friends were standing around in the parking lot. They were tan, like surfers. They wore Abercrombie shirts and khaki shorts, ankle socks and shell necklaces. There seemed to be dozens of them.

"Come on," Rachel said. She got out, opened Greg's door. "Come. Greg. Let me introduce."

"Wait," Greg said. He realized again that he should not be doing this. "I have to do something... with my car." Things would be said. Why didn't Greg have friends his own age? Where were his peers? Why wasn't he in college or something? Was he a pervert? If not, what was he? Greg rattled the keys in the ignition, as if there were something irregular and needy about his car that required this rattling—to appease the engine, maybe, which might otherwise refuse to work. He turned the ignition on. Then he turned it off. What was he doing? He had the somewhat comforting thought that he could go home now. Go home, eat bacon, watch The History Channel.

"Okay." Rachel was squinting at him and grinning. "Wait here then. I'll be right back." She walked away.

Greg focused outward—something a book had told him to do, a calming technique: you pretended you didn't exist; if something didn't exist it couldn't be worried about. In the parking lot, entire families were exiting their minivans and moving in clusters toward Wal-Mart. They all looked pasty and hopeless, and somehow squandered, or else in the process of squandering. They looked obese. Even the skinny ones looked obese. Greg thought about this. Then Rachel was back, with a friend, who stuck his hand through Greg's open window.

"I'm Steve," he said. They shook hands and Steve said, "Looks like we'll be working together tonight, eh?"

Greg nodded.

Steve stooped and looked past Greg, at Rachel, who had sat down in the passenger seat. He gave Rachel double thumbs up and a wink so unnatural that it momentarily paralyzed Greg, then sat in back.

"Let's go," Rachel said. "Make a left at the light. Then another left. I'll tell you what to do. I'll *directionalize* you."

"Why don't I just let you drive?" Greg said. He thought it might sound carefree, slacken things up or something. But he didn't get the inflection right. It sounded like, "Why don't *you* drive then, since you know everything and are an asshole."

Rachel looked at Greg a moment. She smiled. Greg felt his neck stiffen up. He stared outside at an overturned shopping cart. A ratty-haired girl kicked at it, then ran away.

Steve leaned forward between the front seats. "You don't want Rachel driving," he said. "How about I drive?" He looked at Greg, at Rachel, back at Greg. He had a buzz cut and a head like a horse, though handsome. A handsome horse.

Steve got out and so did Greg. They bumped into each other as they went to switch seats. Steve patted Greg's shoulder and told him not to worry. Greg sat in back, feeling dazed and centerless.

Steve moved his head around and talked loudly while driving. He pointed like a mock-tourist guide at things. "Where I ran out on my check," he said, pointing at Denny's. "They didn't cook my chicken fingers all the way. They served me raw chicken! Then they offered me one free thing from their shitty 99-cent desert value menu or whatever, like that would make up for risking my life. Denny's is alright though." He went on like this for a while, then all of a sudden wanted to know about Greg. "So you went to college. Then what, you couldn't handle it?"

Steve's loudness made Greg feel a bit comfortable, though in a fatalistic way. Steve wasn't a human being; he was a human *machine*, in the front seat, making noises, driving a car. What would happen was that this Steve-machine would make noises and drive cars for a number of years, then one day stop.

"No," Greg said. "The tuition was out of my league." He began to make things up. The truth was he did the four years without making any friends. Actually he did make a few friends, but within weeks they all changed, in his view, somehow, into enemies. And after the second year, then, he stopped trying, as it was nearly impossible to make friends unless you already had some. Though probably he had never tried in the first place, or ever. He felt this way sometimes, that he'd never in his life tried at anything. Probably, like some people didn't know how to swim, Greg didn't know the meaning of the word *try*. "Someone gave me TB," he said, "on top of it all." He made a thing up, then tacked on a cliché—so it would sound natural, or something.

Rachel turned around, grinning. She didn't have her seatbelt on and now she put it on and turned back around. "Someone gave you a TV!"

TAO LIN

"TB," Steve said. "Tuberculosis, dummy." He made eye contact with Greg in the rearview mirror. "Then what? You never went back? How's your lung?"

"They gave me a TB scholarship, but I told them to go to hell," Greg said. His voice was unintentionally monotone and grim and mumbled, a kind of misanthropic drone. He sounded like he didn't want to talk anymore, didn't want to be bothered.

"What was that?" Steve said.

Greg hesitated. "Nothing," he said. Then there was a long, woozy silence. Things were changing in this silence, Greg felt. Tact was taking its clothes off and belching, reaching for the remote. This is what happened, Greg knew, what always happened. You did things—you tried, maybe—but after you did one thing you had to wait a while before you could do another thing. You had to sit in a waiting room where the magazines were non-profit and frank, without gloss or pictures, but only rectangular article after article on why it—other people, communication, life generally—just was not worth it. You were bored, so you read them all. The receptionist was friendly but behind glass and on the phone. The ceiling fan had one blade. It spun around, slow, like a chainsaw. By the time they called your name, you did not want to move. You had given up. You went out the other door, got in your car, punched the steering wheel, drove to McDonald's, ordered something with extra, extra, extra bacon; and you didn't say "please." You said, "I want extra bacon on it." You said that again, to make sure.

"How's your lung?" Steve said. "Are you at 80% capacity or whatever?" He twisted around very fast and looked at Greg.

Greg shrugged.

"How's *your* lung?" Rachel asked Steve, who peered hard at the control panel, then turned the air-conditioner on full blast. "Yeah, I thought so," Rachel said. She moved her face right up to the air-conditioner grate.

They passed Greg's old elementary school—a flat, starfishy thing, expanded over the years in a makeshift and unenergetic way, with portables and pavilions. In third grade, on the way to P.E., Greg had spit on a minivan, due to peer pressure. Someone tattled on him and he was sent to the Principal's office. The Principal asked why he did it, then gave him detention.

"TB makes me think of inner tubes," Rachel said. "Poisonous ones that if you use them you get rashes." She laughed. "Tubular colossus," she said. "Sounds like… something."

"Rachel," Steve said. He paused. "Hey, I went to Wet 'N Wild the other day. This lady was with her son. It was hilarious."

"What was hilarious?" Rachel said.

"Your *mom* was ridiculous." Steve yawned. He laughed a little.

"That was stupid," Rachel said. She punched at Steve's side. "I said what was *hilarious*, anyway, not ridiculous. Thanks for listening."

"I said hilarious *first*," Steve said. He seemed to think about that. "Greg," he then said. "Sorry you have to witness our stupidity."

"No," Greg said. He leaned forward a little. "Thank you." Something had gone wrong. Greg had mixed-up apology and appreciation, and maybe some other things. He didn't quite understand it.

"Hmm," Steve said. "You are welcome." He pointed at a Starbucks that had recently opened. But he didn't say anything. Then he said, "So Greg. Did you roll houses a lot in your high school days?"

Greg wanted to be enthusiastic, wanted to be friendly and quick with anecdotes—here was another opportunity!—but, as often happened to him in small talk, he now forgot everything that he ever knew. Information rushed away from him, became distant and twinkling as the cosmos. "A little," he said. In the outer space of his head, he floated upside-down and sideways, like an astronaut—safety cord severed.

"How many times?" Steve said. "Thirty?"

Greg tried to think of what to say, but couldn't decide. Too much time passed. He made eye contact with Rachel in the rearview mirror and then looked quickly, wildly, away.

"We're pros," Rachel said. "We do this, what, twice a week? We did our school. We did this tree one time. A tree in the middle of nowhere, in this field. Someone was like, we should roll that tree, and everyone agreed immediately."

Greg leaned back into his seat, looked out the window, made eye contact with a little girl in another car, and then looked down into his own lap.

"Yeah; it is kind of sad," Steve said. "This is all we do really. Not sad. Funny. For a while we did fireworks, drove around lighting fireworks, tossing them out of the car. That was fun. Before that, what was before that?"

"Truth or dare," Rachel said. "Remember truth or dare?"

Greg remembered truth or dare. One time, Crystal Kendle dared him to jump off the roof. Either jump off the roof or kiss her. Greg was nine and wanted to kiss her. But he climbed a ladder to the roof and jumped off and hurt his ankles. The other kids called him stupid. Crystal Kendle went to the same high school as Greg, but they were strangers by then. She was one of those willowy, surrounded girls. Always surrounded, always willowy. Greg was one of those kids who, to avoid being seen eating alone, never sat in the cafeteria; was always carrying his lunch around, like someone lost or eccentric, looking for a safe place. He invariably ate in spots weird and badly-lit, spots ruthless with indignity— a dewy nook; an abstract, long-forgotten bench; an inexplicable room adjacent the bathroom, with prison bars instead of a door.

Steve turned the car into a neighborhood. A squirrel ran across the street. Steve said to be quiet. He pointed at a house. "There's Ali's home," he said loudly. "Probably in bed already. Sleeping." He laughed. "I don't even know why that's funny. I really don't."

"Do you know Ali?" Greg said.

"We're not best friends but yeah, I guess I know him," Steve said. "He goes to our school. He plays tennis. He's probably Indian, judging by his name. But this isn't a racial thing. It's just chance, you know, coincidence or whatever. Ali's a good guy. He's alright. I bet he plays tennis a lot, though, like four hours a day."

"I told Justin we were rolling his house sometime this week," Rachel said. "He said he had a paintball gun and would hide in the bushes. He was being all serious for some reason." She laughed. "He was like, 'Do it, if you have to,' all serious-like."

"Excellent," Steve said. "We'll do his house after. His home."

Greg had the thought that "Justin" was codename for "Greg"—for himself. That they were going to roll *his* place next. And he'd do it too, he knew, he'd roll his own apartment—like some convoluted, surreal attempt at allegory—and to avoid embarrassment he'd pretend vehemently that he didn't know it was his own apartment; he'd change his identity if he had to—lawfully, with forms, a fifty-dollar processing fee.

They came to a cul-de-sac. Two other cars were parked in the street.

Steve parked, got out.

"Whose car?" someone asked Steve.

"Mine," Steve said. "I carjacked it."

"Bullshit."

"Greg's." Steve pointed at the car.

"Who's 'Greg'?"

"I don't know," Steve said. He laughed. "Some guy. He had TB."

"It's so early," someone else was saying. "It's barely even dark out." His voice took on a mock-authoritative tone. "We are becoming too confident, we rowdy teenagers, we, um, fucking...."

In the car, Greg and Rachel were still and silent until Rachel twisted abruptly around and looked at Greg, her eyes wide and white and steady. "Do you really like rolling? Do you like it a lot?" She wasn't smiling, but looked actually a little bored. But then she was grinning and looked giddy.

Greg scratched his neck. "I guess," he said. His voice came out little, then gone, like a leprechaun. He began to look around. There was a sudden erratic gravity to his eyes; there were people in there—little people, with little rocket packs.

"Do you like Steve?"

"I don't know," Greg said. He looked down at his hands, which he moved toward one another, then touched, and held, like gimp lovers. His thumbs were closest to him. He thought of twiddling them.

"Do you like *me*?"

Something fat and sweaty entered Greg, did a crude little jig, and then vanished, leaving in its place a hotness, a plain and glowless burning; Greg was embarrassed for many different reasons that came all at once—the accidental mob of them crowding in, drunk and with pitchforks, demanding answers. "I don't know," Greg said. "No." He meant to say yes, or something like that, but "No" was what came out, and it came out mean, and his face looked mean, too, like it always did.

Rachel grinned, but Greg didn't see. He was looking down into the dark area where his shoes were. He felt as if in grade school, and he had a thought, that he wasn't *ready* to like anyone yet, that he was far from it.

Someone called Rachel's name and she exited the car. Greg sat a moment, thought about things, then got out too, feeling like a wasteland of things gone wrong, an entire country of wrongness. He couldn't see Rachel again—he wouldn't—not her or anyone she knew. He would have to quit at the library, maybe move to another county or state. He went to the trunk of his car and tore open a 24-pack of toilet paper, took a roll, and threw it madly, almost horizontally, into a tree. It went clear through, and then over a fence. Greg got another roll. Someone laughed and told Greg that it was the wrong house. Besides Greg, there were about a dozen teenagers. They took their rolls, dashed a few houses down to Ali's house, and started hurling them up. They wrapped individual flower plants and laid toilet paper carefully on the tops of hedges. One girl unfurled her roll, taut, from a tree in Ali's yard to a mailbox across the street. A car came by. Everyone hid half-assedly behind bushes and trees. The car slowed a little, then accelerated and left. Rolling resumed. Someone said he didn't think this was Ali's house. They spread out, began rolling the houses on either side. Greg was in a side yard, where no one could see him. He threw his roll up into a tree, scrambled over the grass, and caught it on its way down; and for a moment felt that he knew again what it was to be a kid—to be four, five years old—but the feeling passed, went through him like a little dream, like a dream a baby rabbit would have. When they had no more toilet paper, they ran into the street and stood a moment to admire. Toilet paper curtained the houses, undulating and in layers, like something undersea and unlikely, and promising; stray sections of toilet paper stuck airily against branches and shingles, lay pat and torn and strewn over the yards and bushes; wrapped-up flower plants sat like little gifts on the grass, squat and cabbage-like, bandaged and decapitated as heads. In a different world, these houses would be celebrated. People would dance in the yards, sleep the night outside. In this world, there would be form-letter warnings from the neighborhood community association, and if the lawns were not cleaned by the next afternoon, calls would have to be made. Everyone ran wildly back into their cars, laughing and screaming things. Steve sat in the driver's seat, Greg sat in back, and Rachel sat passenger. There was another kid, also, in back. He was smiling and looking at Greg and he said, "Who are you?"

Greg said his name, but in an unaccompanied sort of voice—a voice de-personed early-on, in the brain. The new kid kept looking at him. Greg wondered if he had answered, or just mouthed something, no sound coming out. His heart was beating fast. The question stayed in his head—*who are you*? "I'm Greg," he said, but his voice seemed now so loud and melodramatic that he felt only Greglike, not truly Greg. He felt Greggy; and he felt dizzy and hollow and aloft, like an attic—a family of owls inside and hoo'ing, or else outside and flapping—mauling—at the roof. The new kid said, "You had TB!" and made a face. Greg felt that he was blushing hard and that Rachel was looking at him and he turned away, looked out his window. Down the road, someone was walking a dog, and above that was the low, thin, whiteblue moon—slit and off-color as something about to be sealed shut from the other side.

They drove off. Toilet paper caught against Greg's window, rippled there like a flag, and then rushed off and away. All the strange and giant things began to float by, outside, in the night, and from another car, someone stuck their head out their window and screamed, "Faggot Ali!" Someone else screamed, "Muhammad Ali!" And someone else, "Muhammad Ali Baba! Ahhh! *Ahhhhrrrrr*!"

Sincerity

Once, while having sex with his girlfriend Alicia, the theme from Star Wars had gone into Aaron's head and he had suddenly and loudly begun to hum it, which he could not, then, sustain, as he had started to laugh.

He laughed and laughed.

And things changed after that.

Sex became a precarious thing. Often, it could not happen. Songs or tunes, little ditties—tom-tom drum beats, kazoo-y cartoon music—would automatically go into both their heads. The required focus and grave seriousness of sex, that inner, outer-spacey concentration toward some black and scrappy source, some vague but findable piece of lust—it could not happen anymore. Only songs could happen. And there were other changes. Their quarrels—they had always fought—took on a tone of mocking and farce. Sometimes, now, fighting with Alicia, both of them yelling—shrieking at times, and crying, even, like babies!—something in Aaron would scald white and clean, like a flash pasteurization, and he would tickle her until she fell down giggling. Or he would just start laughing, then have to chase down and tickle her, to sort of convince her—delude her—of his otherwise unacceptable behavior. And Alicia, too, underwent change, having once, during a fight, opened a drawer and taken from it a glass of water—she had premeditated it!—and, after telling Aaron, sincerely, that he was an asshole, grinned and poured the water on his head.

This new flippancy, though, was not strictly joke-y and fun. There was something, Aaron felt, murderous to it. In each moment of laughter or play there was a small probability of manslaughter, a percentage chance of violence and jail-time. Alicia sometimes went too far, Aaron felt. She cut him once with a fork. Another time, Aaron daydreamed for a very long time about setting a death-trap for Alicia; a spiked pit, perhaps, in some parking lot—a death pit!

In this way, then—unable to assimilate these feelings of assassination, farce, song, and play—they became a bit reckless. They grew daring and confused. Though their fights increased noticeably in frequency and lies when they spent more than one consecutive night together, and though, Aaron knew, they did not really love each other, not anymore, maybe not ever (they had become like siblings now, except that they lacked the responsibility of family, that kind of forced love, and so were less siblings than just sort of moody, interdepartmental co-workers)—though, in other words, they really should not have been getting an apartment together, they went ahead and got an apartment together, signed a two-year lease, as, in addition to their new brazenness, they were not—and had never been—energetic people, but were, to be honest, needy people; prone to disillusionment, lazy about new things, and very much fearful of loneliness, desperation, meaninglessness, and dating. They needed each other, they knew, needed the vague momentum of two, the mild tyranny and oppression of it—that second brain like an orbital satellite and remote control to the first brain—to let them know what, at any given moment, was the point in life; and also to argue with and complain to.

Their new apartment was sunny and spacey in an atomic-bombed way. It had wood floors. It was on the edge of a massive, abandoned, wasp-infested shopping center plaza, a few miles from the university. It was a dry place, with no cockroaches or mildew, but many spiders and moths and silverfish—bugs that were better than other people's bugs, Aaron liked to say, were wittier and more role-playing; sometimes, on the weekends, two large spiders would walk out into the center of the bedroom and stay there for hours, like henchmen; then when no one was looking, usually during the night, they would hurry away, like lovers.

In bed, they watched a moth walk experimentally across the floor, taking small, tottering steps.

"How funny," Alicia said. "So funny."

"It's like a little... brown bear," Aaron said. "A tiny one, because of the fuzziness."

"I can see that," Alicia said. "That's kind of scary. I imagine it turning into a bear."

The moth walked slowly out of view, behind a desk, then—back in view, going faster now—into the bathroom, where it lifted and flew noisily around, steady and aimed, and fulfilled, Aaron thought distractedly, as a miniature blow-dryer. They were talking now about spring break. Someone had brought up what to do over spring break. Who, though? This seemed to matter. Aaron had a feeling that, depending on who had brought it up, he should be either apprehensive or relieved.

"Maybe we should go to London," Alicia said.

"London has no literary value," Aaron said. Though his face was turned away, he sort of forced a grin anyway. He hated it when people got so inured that they went around being sarcastic without ever changing their facial expression. It was inhuman. It was so cheaply disenchanted. There was no compassion to going around meanly making jokes in people's faces. Though, Aaron didn't like it when comedians laughed at their own jokes. It was too... human, or something.

"They have Stonehedge. Stone... thing," Alicia was saying. "Stone*henge*. I have this fantasy... of living inside of Stonehenge. I know it's not a house." They didn't say anything for a while. "*You* have no literary value," Alicia then said.

"You have no face value," Aaron said. He laughed. "I didn't mean anything by that. Why did I say that?"

"Face value," Alicia said.

"Because your face is ugly. That's why I said it." Aaron rolled over, grinning, and looked at Alicia. "Really, though. It's because of the idiom or whatever. What's the face value of this rare coin I found in my backyard? See." He looked at her a moment more— looked at her face; her two eyes, black and incremental as a Japanese animation, her nose and mouth like well-made trinkets; how could anything true and complex ever be expressed?—and then rolled her carefully over and held her, loosely, like a thing that needed comfort, but also needed air. Alicia didn't say anything. It was only October, Aaron knew. They probably shouldn't have been talking about spring break. It was elliptic, foreboding talk. It assumed certain things about winter break.

"Who started talking about spring break first?" Aaron said. "A minute ago."

"What," Alicia said. She had a habit of automatically saying 'what.' Sometimes she'd say 'what' and then respond immediately after—cynically, without any visible shame. But it was a good way to buy time, Aaron had to admit, a cautious, maybe even considerate, thing to do. Probably it started that way, as a conversational strategy, but now just continued as a thing of her identity—a crucial part of her identity! Aaron felt some contempt for her. He felt bigoted and tired. He wasn't going to repeat his question.

"What," Alicia said again, after a while.

"'What' what," Aaron said.

They didn't talk for a long time, did not move, just lay in bed. Eventually, then, they made it somehow into the kitchen, and from there, affected no doubt by sunlight, they became a bit zealous and drove to a movie theatre and watched two movies, then ate dinner, slowly and dully, without drinking any water—feeling sort of shadowy and eradicated after the movies—and were now back in bed. Neither of them had spoken for a long time. Aaron was feeling very complacent, falling asleep a little. There were times when he stopped thinking—his cares and concerns left him, in a faraway smoke; a smoke he could see, in the distance—and everything around him stayed the same, so that he then just sort of passed, one-dimensionally—time-wise—through it all, feeling honest and fine and worriless.

"Do you want to know what I'm thinking about?" Alicia said. But Aaron had fallen asleep. Alicia waited a minute, then woke Aaron and repeated herself.

"What are you thinking about?" Aaron really wanted to know. Sleep had made him curious about Alicia. He had forgotten her, and would now relearn her. He felt grateful and intimate.

"I've been worried," Alicia said. "Can't you tell?"

Aaron now wondered why she hadn't asked what *he* was thinking about. It seemed maybe hypocritical, what was happening right now, seemed almost—somehow—adulterous. "My sister hates me," Alicia said; she and her sister had been close until Alicia left for college; now Alicia was worried; she felt guilty, and urgent, as time was running out, she felt, for reconciliation—and then there were some intricacies that Aaron had never fully understood. He had heard this talk before. He began to wonder if they ever resolved that thing with the face value; and there was something about spring break. What was that? Aaron realized that he wasn't listening to Alicia at all, was not even trying. He could hear her voice, but was somehow able to process it not as language but as sound. He laughed. "Wait," he said, interrupting her, "what are you saying right now? Sorry, I wasn't listening." He laughed again. "Can you start over, please?"

"Should I make her a card? What should I write on it, though," Alicia said. Aaron was losing concentration again—so fast, he thought factually—was thinking about a story he had been working on, but then Alicia's voice became suddenly very loud. "You've got to stop doing that," she said. "You can't just *phase out* like that. That's so rude. Do you know how rude that is?"

"I know," Aaron said. "Sorry. I'm really sorry. I know it's really rude. I really am sorry." He was. But should he be apologizing this vehemently? It felt mindless and insincere. "You do it too," he said. He didn't know this for a fact, but it was a good, vague thing to say, probably. There was a long moment of silence, and then he tickled her; she tensed and got quickly out of bed.

She walked to the bathroom door, slowly turned around, came back to the bed, and lay down.

"I'm going to sleep," she said, but then got out of bed again, left the room, and came back with a steak knife, held by her head, like to attack. She walked to Aaron and stabbed him in the chest. The blade was flimsy, Aaron saw. Plastic. He laughed. "I'm serious," Alicia said. She was grinning. "I'm kind of angry." She threw the knife across the room, where it fell on a shirt, from which a silverfish darted out, stopped, and then glided slowly into the bathroom.

Alicia lay down facing away. "Did you like that?" she said. "It wasn't just for fun." She pulled the covers up, tight, to her chin. "Don't worry. I'll get over this," she said. "I'm just sleepy. I'm just worried about my sister. Nothing's wrong." Lately, they were always reassuring each other that nothing was wrong; and probably it was true—life wasn't supposed to be incredible, after all. Life wasn't some incredible movie. Life was all the movies, ever, happening at once. There were good ones, bad ones, some went straight to video. This seemed right. That's exactly, literally, right, Aaron thought, already mocking himself. He could not sleep and began to worry about his parents. They were always yelling at each other, about the stock market. They stayed home every day and had no friends. Actually, they did go to the movies every week; they did that. Still, there was something disastrous about them; that they had only each other, as they were immigrants and so had no relatives nearby; or that they didn't seem to have any hobbies, or interests, even. They were incomprehensible to Aaron. He was, though, writing a story about them, whatever that meant.

He had an idea one day, to switch into Alicia's writing workshop. He would surprise her or something. He was lazy to do the official switching, so one day he just affected an air of having switched—something of ironic efficacy, of recent bureaucratic struggle overcome, he guessed—and then went in, a little blank in the face, prepared to blame the registrar. But no one said anything, not even Alicia.

"Aaron, yay," she had said, actually; but that was all.

A few weeks later, they were discussing Aaron's story; not the one about his parents—he was still working on that one, as it had changed on him, taken on a made-for-TV movie tone, which a story could do—but a different one; not a serious story, but one that Aaron was proud of. He had worked very hard on making it impervious to criticism.

"This has no literary value," Alicia said, after some generic praise from the class.

"*You* have no literary value," Aaron said. "You as a person."

"That's so good," someone said softly.

"You're quoting me," Alicia said. "Everyone; he just quoted me." She had been depressed lately, she had been telling Aaron once or twice per week. ("You're not depressed," Aaron would say. "If you're depressed so am I. We both are.") She was thinking about quitting school, moving back home, up north. She worried about her parents and mildly retarded brother; and her sister, who had stayed home, seven years now, rather than go to college.

"You're quoting *me*," Aaron said. It was his word against hers, he knew, though probably they shouldn't be quarrelling in class like this. But he was grinning, so probably it wasn't quarrelling—probably the grinning made it okay.

"College... has no literary value," someone said. The class was an incisive one, though in a meek and circuitous way, as they were shy people, really—fearful, above all, Aaron knew, of the stupid remark, the trite sentiment; always coming in late to avoid small talk; the dreaded small talk!—though, depending on mood, and on drugs, no doubt, they could get a bit wild, as they all had good senses of humor and playful spirits (after reading D.H. Lawrence's *The Blind Man* the previous week, they had laughed and laughed at D.H.'s use of a mollusk simile; the lawyer who was *like a mollusk whose shell is broken*).

"What about community college?" the teacher said. "I think those have literary value."

"Community colleges with minority make-ups have literary value," Aaron said. He remembered something; a few days ago he had joked about community colleges—condescendingly, Alicia had thought; and then they fought—had said something about the vague leper colonies of them. "Community colleges on the west coast have beach value."

"Littoral value," Alicia said slowly. Aaron looked at her.

"Well then, what's more important," the teacher said. "Literary value, or beach value? Compare and contrast. Two pages, choose your own font, due next week." The teacher claimed to believe that no one would write anything of importance between the ages of fifteen and forty. He was not very attentive in class—sometimes letting discussion dwindle into woozy, melancholy, time-distorting silences; sometimes getting up casually to use the restroom, like a student!—but was really good at taking sarcasm to the next level, which the class found idiosyncratic and refreshing and really liked, a lot.

They drove two hours to visit Aaron's parents one day.

Aaron's mother was sitting in the living room, blushing, crying a little. The TV was on. Aaron's father was in the computer room. He said that Aaron's mother had just lost $20,000 by shorting the wrong stock. He was hunched close to the computer, and did not look angry, but nervous, or else giddy—it was hard to tell.

"They always fight about the same things," Aaron said in bed. "They're not in love. Not even close. Actually, I don't know. I don't know anything. All I know is I'm worried about them. All I know's I have this image of a swamp and it's rising up and moving into me, like a fog. I read about swamp-fogs. Swamp gas. They rise up and move and people think they're spaceships. Will-o'-the-wisp. That sounds like a toilet paper for elves. Upper class elves." He felt excited. Being with Alicia in a large house in his childhood bed excited him for some reason. He really was worried, though.

"Your dad on the computer, he was like a mad-scientist," Alicia said.

"They have money but never spend it. All they do is lose it in the stock market." Aaron laughed. "They're so bad at the stock market. What is the stock market anyway? A computer or what? It's like an idea or something. It's probably an entire country. Some tiny country between Mongolia and China, with a rainbow-colored force-field around it." He thought about that and felt a bit nostalgic. He kind of wanted to move to that place. "And what's *gravity*? No one knows. No one cares. Why is there gravity? That's so weird. That's like, why are there things? That's so depressing, that that question even exists. But sincere, I think. I mean I don't feel fake at all, asking that. Finally, I don't feel fake!" He had talked too long, he knew. He wouldn't talk anymore. Alicia would talk. Or she wouldn't. Aaron had the feeling that she was devoting little to no attention to him while worrying secretly and intensely about other things. "Are you thinking about your sister?"

"You and I always fight about the same things too," Alicia said.

"We're working on it though," Aaron said. They were. They had even come up with a plan, that whenever one of them started to get angry, the other would let them know—show them how useless it was—and then they would hold each other. "We have the plan." He laughed. Actually, he had come up with the plan; it had been his idea!

"What are you so happy about?" Alicia said.

"I'm not," Aaron said. "I'm actually really, really, really worried." He tickled Alicia until she fell off the bed, onto the carpet, from where she crawled to the bathroom. They were getting lazy. They weren't trying anymore. Alicia shouldn't be crawling like that, Aaron thought slowly, that's strange and unhappy. He waited for her, but fell asleep.

For some time now Aaron had been writing every day. There were moments when he felt sudden blots of something—truth? serotonin? worse, cholesterol?—in his head, new and startling things, and he'd resolve them into words, and there would be some complicated, ulterior, and life-affirming, he suspected, pleasure in that; and he even felt, sometimes, the somewhat comforting beginnings, maybe, of something like a career. But he had certain disillusionments about writing that he felt he could not ignore. He didn't like the subjectivity of it. He liked a thing to be perfect and meticulous and all-encompassing and, finally, unchangeable—unworryable. But there were, he knew, only momentary perfections, which were not perfections at all, but delusions. It worried him. Could one delude oneself through a life? Yes, he knew. Probably that was the only way.

But Aaron was not good at delusion. He had, in his life, he suspected, learned something, grasped some knowledge—in a once and random, adolescent way, like chicken pox, or else in a worked-at way, like a skill; probably somehow both—that prevented him from moving entirely into the delusion of a thing. And he had learned this something very early in his life, he knew, as he could not remember ever having really believed in anything. Not in religion, which made him restless, the cul-de-sac of it, how it turned you around a little, patted you on the head, held block parties in celebration of itself; not in society, with its earnest system of nonexistence, how it existed, really, in the unhappened future, in progress and realization; and not in himself, as what did it mean to believe in oneself—wasn't that just a sneaky way of proclaiming yourself God? It was, and Aaron especially did not believe in anything as vague and clichéd—and with as many capitalization rules—as God.

Yet he nevertheless had always been able to play along, to live mostly contently, he guessed, and sanely— as he had a small talent for meaningfulness, for patching together cultural units and other people's beliefs into his own makeshift sensibilities and short-term convictions. He could take a thing from the world and fold it over, like a handkerchief, make a little wad of it, and then pack it inside of his own heart, as a staunching thing, a temporary absorber of new blood, a thing to pump and pool into—honestly and without too much cynicism—and it was in this way that he was okay, he felt, at living; he was pretty good at it, probably as good as he would ever be.

In class they discussed Aaron's story about his parents, which Aaron had given up on, leaving in, among other things that should've been cut, a non-sequitur about the mother's son feeling *fluttering and doomed as a hummingbird with a spinal disease* and a description of the father's head that was intended to imply worry but instead implied, if anything, Aaron knew, cold-slice bologna—*his pocked and boyish eyes stuck like salt-washed olives in the peppered meat of his face*. It was called "Eddy," which was the name of the son in the story. Aaron had wanted to avoid in the title irony, cleverness, smugness, frivolousness, profundity, melodrama, condescension; and had ended up not with sincerity, he felt, but a woozy, resounding sort of tonelessness and maybe a little—or possibly a lot of—irony.

"This is a serious story," Aaron said. It was. Or at least he had wanted it to be. Or rather, he didn't want the class to assume it was parody, which they would otherwise do. If anything, it was satire. Though truthfully, Aaron knew, it was probably less a story than twenty pages of failed sentences, a few of which worked, if precariously, as jokes.

"Serious," said the teacher. "What do you mean?"

"I don't know. When I wrote it... I had this mean look on my face. I had a piece of paper taped on the computer screen that had all the synonyms for 'existence' written on it." He didn't want to talk about his story anymore. He wanted to talk about existence. What was it? What was to be done about it?

"I looked up existence the other day," someone said. "A synonym for it—the internet said—was the word 'something.' I didn't get that."

"'Something' can be a synonym for everything," Alicia said. "Anything."

"Good insight," the teacher said. He smiled a bit wildly at Alicia.

"Good job, Alicia," someone said, and began to clap. Other people clapped. Some people stood, and soon everyone was standing and applauding, Aaron the loudest. His story felt puny now; felt, in a distanced and forgiven way, sort of perfected—it was but a moment in all the others, a single squishy, lopsided beating of some imperfect but trying heart; a happened and unfixable thing.

After the standing ovation, someone said something about D.H. Lawrence and clams and everyone laughed. There was a long and pleasant silence, everyone smiling, and then someone asked Aaron if he had read Antonya Nelson; she wrote about families too. Someone else said something about Nelson Mandela, and then talked about his own life—his crazy life!—for quite some time, which could sometimes happen, usually near the end of a class, and was looked upon by classmates not with contempt, but with sympathy and understanding; sometimes you just needed to talk about yourself for five or ten minutes straight.

Alicia's story was workshopped a few weeks later, around Thanksgiving.

She was a strict autobiographical writer, not even changing names. It made the class alert and, at first, preachy—they could critique her actual life, her flawed and disgusting life!—but then hesitant and depressed, as who in the class knew how to live their own life? Who could say what was better for Alicia, what was wrong and how to change?

"Why does Aaron stay with Alicia if he doesn't love her really," Aaron said. They had become very open with one another recently, had both admitted, among other things that made them nervous, having wished sudden and accidental deaths onto their parents, as they were both fearful and unwanting of what would otherwise happen—their parents would still die, of course, eventually, but what before that? Fifteen years of Alzheimer's? Dementia? Cancer? Aaron and Alicia felt they would not be able to deal with any of those. It had brought them closer, Aaron felt. In the farness of their worrying—the tedious escape of it, how it shuttled you slowly away from real life, into a sort of deep space—they had come, truly, closer to each other, in an echoed, gaping-expanse-between-them way. Or not. Probably not.

"He isn't really staying with her, I think. He's more just not leaving her," someone said. "There was that thing about a two-year lease. They signed a two-year lease."

"What do people think about Alicia," Alicia said. "Should she move home?" Before leaving for college, she had helped her sister take care of their brother, who, Aaron learned—with vague recognition—from the story, was a bit abnormal due to sleeping pills he was given as an infant. *Alicia felt poisoned and covered in nets, like in a fishing net with poisonous starfish and things in it,* said the story. She was not a good writer. Though, actually, Aaron really liked that line. It had an alien, adolescent charm to it.

"Alicia's sister should realize that family is arbitrary," someone said. "Alicia's realized, so her sister should too. That would solve things. Plus it's true, objectively. I'm just stating facts right now, like a computer."

"What has Alicia realized?" Alicia said. "Be more specific."

"I disagree with that," Aaron said. "Everyone should realize that everything is arbitrary, and so nothing is—which is also true—and so everyone should try and be nice to their family, in the way that everyone should be maximally nice to everyone." Start with your family, Aaron thought without much conviction, that's what a person needed to do—that was the given task, probably, the world's free and weary advice—and from there, then, spread out from family to include, gradually, everyone else. "I'm profound," he said aloud, by accident, but effectively, as some people laughed.

"Is it important Alicia's parents are immigrants?" Alicia said. Her parents, like Aaron's, had, for whatever reason—neither of them knew exactly why—left (escaped?) their families and friends for a new, relativeless, friendless, equally middle-class, less communicable place; a place, maybe, with less worries?

"You didn't explore that," someone said. "That's not your focus. *Or is it?*"—people had gotten more sarcastic and long-winded as the semester went along; without their shyness, actually, Aaron suspected, they were all jerks—"Ignoring it, that may be a political statement. *Maybe.* Not to say you have an agenda. Not to say you're running for office."

"What do you mean by political?" Alicia said. "What are you talking about?"

"Politics," said the teacher. "Social relations involving authority or power."

"I meant if it's important as to what people... should do," Alicia said. "I'm not talking about social power." She had changed, Aaron knew. She used to be happy, maybe. Now she was just distracted and incomprehensible all the time.

"Alicia should do drugs," someone said. "Then her family can worry about her and she won't have to worry anymore. And later she can write a raw, unflinching, but ultimately redemptive novel or memoir about it."

"Alicia should be like a crustacean whose shell has been bludgeoned," Aaron said. Everyone laughed, though in an exerted way, with many enunciated "ha-ha's"; the mollusk thing was getting old. Though maybe Aaron was mocking exactly that. Yeah, he thought, he was.

"Alicia's so detached and melodramatic," someone else said. "She sort of isn't believable. I don't believe she exists—as a real person. Why would anyone sign a two-year lease? I don't believe that. Which is okay, though. I mean, Moby Dick, yeah, that's really believable. Not that I liked Moby Dick. I didn't. I mean, I didn't read it. Never mind though. Sorry. I don't know what I'm talking about. I'm just... stupid. Please don't listen to me. Okay."

"She's like a green mussel that's been eaten so there's just the shell left," Aaron said. He was very quietly and completely ignored, which could sometimes happen in a workshop; he was not embarrassed at first, but a little bit proud—his joke was simply too true and complex (too good) to be acknowledged—then he was embarrassed.

"Do you exist, Alicia?" the teacher said. "If you don't, then you don't have to answer that."

"What the hell are you talking about?" Alicia said.

It was getting uncomfortable. Everyone stared not at Alicia, but at their own hands, or else abstractly at some piece of table or wall, as there had become in the room a feeling of immobilization, something of both nostalgia and doom—a sort of gigantic helplessness that could take affect, sometimes, near the end of class; everyone feeling elderly and pointless from all the criticism and subsequent qualifications and admittances of not knowing anything—an unpleasant urge to stay still for a very long time, for *ever*, perhaps, not saying or thinking anything, but just accepting one another, entering and absorbing and maybe, finally, somehow—with anonymity, osmosis, conjecture, and luck—then, experiencing one another.

For winter break they went to Aaron's house.

They fought about how Aaron never went to Alicia's house. "You haven't been back to your house in two years or whatever," Aaron said, "am I supposed to go there by myself?" but then immediately apologized and said that they would go to her house, then, for spring break. He had almost no anger these days, and he hugged her and apologized two more times.

With Aaron's parents, they went to a theme park, the movies.

On New Year's Eve, in a large-windowed restaurant atop a pier at the beach, his parents fought about the stock market. Aaron's father called Aaron's mother stupid; she told him to stop acting like a baby. They had spoken English at first, so that Alicia could understand, but had gotten lazy after an hour or so and now spoke only Mandarin.

"A ten point gain is better than a ten percent gain. That's what she thinks," Aaron's father said to Aaron. "That's how her mind works."

"That's right, I'm the stupid one," Aaron's mother said. "He likes stupid girls of course. It gives him a feeling of superiority, a feeling he can't live without." She sat up very straight. "He lost forty-thousand last week," she said loudly to Aaron. "He's a day-trader, a professional."

"Is a ten point gain better than a ten percent gain?" Aaron's father said. He looked down, at an angle, toward Aaron's mother. "Is it?" He had been grinning before, but now his face was red and tense.

Aaron laughed. He liked his parents, and wished, now, sitting here, that they were all the same age and friends, in middle school or something, hanging out. "Calm down," he said. "Don't be so ridiculous. You know she knows it depends on the stock price and is just stubborn to admit you're right. And she knows you know all that, too. The facts are all known. So there's nothing to talk about—argue about." He had just come up with this, but it sounded right, if a bit depressing, as one had, despite falseness or whatever, to be accusatory every once in a while; small talk had to be made, things needed to be said—provocations, sudden risky beliefs and improvisational generalizations—one had to tread water with these preconceptions, these prejudices and quarrels, keep one's head buoyed and in the sun; kick at the dark, wet, worried meaninglessness below.

Aaron's father repeated his question to Aaron's mother. He was grinning again, though tensely.

"Yes," Aaron's mother finally said. "A ten point gain is always better than a ten percent gain." Their entrees came. Aaron's father said something about cooking, at which Aaron's mother put her fork down loudly. She asked for chopsticks, but it was a Cajun restaurant. She looked at her fork and picked it up. She devoured her catfish and then talked at length—looking around the table in a storytelling way—while everyone else ate at a normal speed. She talked in a formal mandarin that Aaron couldn't understand that well. "He meets his young, stupid wife—a person so stupid that here she is now. He has big plans, moves to America. He realizes his big plans. Meanwhile he has his house slave, his cook and child raiser, his nice little affair on the side, his very successful career. He makes a lot of money; he is known in his field. But is he happy? He isn't sure. He wakes in the night. Sweating, panicked. Hungry. But he is a genius and now he is going into retirement, and a genius going into retirement cannot be stopped. I don't know. Listen to me. I don't know." She looked around and then stopped looking around and stared through the window at something outside; a gray and dusty light moved against and off the surface of her eyes, like the wet-dry shine from a cold, unwashed grape. Outside, a gull came into view, floated in place, wobbled, and then pitched back and away, out of control. Aaron laughed a little. Alicia squeezed his hand under the table. Aaron had forgotten she was sitting here, beside him. He had stopped translating for her a long time ago.

Later, at home, Times Square on TV, Aaron's mother apologized, said that Aaron was right about them being stubborn and ridiculous. She patted Aaron's shoulder and smiled at Alicia. On TV, the electrocuted lychee of the New Year's ball—spiked and radioactive as a child's depiction of a thing—ticked smoothly down in imperceptible increments.

The next semester, Aaron—his stories widely rejected by literary magazines—began writing sort of science-fiction conceits for workshop; crude, uncritiqueable things that did not fuck around, but got straight to the point, which was always bafflement. In one, an alien civilization discovers that gravity is the cause of worry, love, and fear, the underlying desire of all things to occupy the same space (to correct the big bang, go against God's, or whoever's, big impulse move, that shady decision of some-thingness) to again become one final, gravityless, unchangeable thing—and is baffled.

He thought it might make a good children's book one day, a collection of them. *Fairy Tales for the Young Disillusionist,* or something. *Handbook for Doomed and/or Disenchanted Children: a Pop-up Collection.*

"I like you," Aaron said in bed. He had begun to like Alicia more each day. She had become quieter and nicer—more lifeless. She felt physically softer. They rarely fought anymore, and when they did it was in a mollified and absent-minded way, with many accidental moments of agreement and overlaps of argument. But they laughed less, too—less loudly—and almost never joked or played, as there was, always, now, the danger of an emotion—any emotion, or even too instantaneous a physical activity—losing sense of itself and then recovering too fast and wrongly, asserting itself as sadness; causing, then, a sort of sourceless, disembodied weeping. They had to be careful of that.

"I like you too," Alicia said. They talked no longer of love, but only of like. Talk of love made them feel banished and of the dark-ages. *Like* was beginning and new; *like* was when you grew wings that made you lithe and interesting; *love* was when those wings kept growing, became thick and unseemly—tarp-like—and then smothered you; wrapped you up, like a bodybag.

Though, still, Aaron kind of wanted to say that he loved her.

"I like you more each day," he said.

"Really."

"I like you more each day, and a lot, overall." Lately, Aaron worried that Alicia would leave him. "Yes, really." She had begun to talk to friends everyday, on her cell phone—friends from high-school. Aaron himself had not kept in touch with friends after high school, though maybe he should have. "I like to hold you," he said. At night, every night now, for twenty or thirty minutes before sleep, Aaron would hold her, from behind, both of them thinking their own things, roundpupiled in the dark, looking out into their bedroom, at all their unseen but no doubt capering bugs, and sometimes forgetting the other person, the conscious, changing life of them, but just holding on to the warm, DNA heap of them.

For spring break, they flew to Alicia's parents' place in New England.

At dinner, at The Olive Garden, Alicia sat by her brother—who seemed, to Aaron, not handicapped, not at all, just a very shy person—but they did not speak to or look at each other. Alicia's parents seemed more like grandparents, and they too did not speak. Only Alicia's sister spoke; she ordered for everyone.

After dinner, in the parking lot, Alicia's brother fell, somehow, into a tree. His face turned a reddish white as he unwrenched his clothing from the branches. In the car, he looked brutalized and war torn. He sat by Aaron and talked to himself. His voice was small and eerie and Aaron tried not to listen to it.

Late that night, Aaron and Alicia walked around her neighborhood. They did not hold hands, but—feeling wild and young from the airdropped newness of the first night in a different state—walked and sometimes ran a little in erratic, separate directions, over strips of grass and sidewalks. The houses were all dark and large and shoebox-shaped. There was a cool, quick movement to the sky above—a cold-watery moonlight, below the clouds but above the rooftops, as between the houses, on the street and lawns where they walked, it was black and still and breezeless.

Aaron thought of living someplace with Alicia. He was not good at meeting people, did not have the skill of escaping his body and so was always drowned in social situations by his own ducts and glands, thwarted by his own nerve-bundles, which would detach somehow and move stupidly into his bloodstream and bump, then, through his heart, and he doubted that, if Alicia left him, he would be able to meet anyone new. They used to, but hadn't for a long time now, discuss moving somewhere together after graduating. Maybe he would bring that up tonight, ask her.

He could see them getting MFAs together, then university teaching jobs, being funny and halfhearted and sometimes extraordinary with students, and somewhere in all this taking care of their parents, into old age and death; and, themselves, then, too, growing old and dying.

As one had to expect very little—almost nothing—from life, Aaron knew, one had to be grateful, not always be trying to seize the days, not like some maniac of living, but to give oneself up, *be seized* by the days, the months and years, be taken up in a froth of sun and moon, some pale and smoothie'd river-cloud of life, a long, drawn-out and gray sort of enlightenment, so that when it was time to die, one did not scream swear words and knock things down, did not make a scene, but went easily, with understanding and tact, and quietly, in a lightly pummeled way, having been consoled—having *allowed* to be consoled—by the soft and generous worthlessness of it all, having allowed to be massaged by the daily beating of life, instead of just beaten.

And Aaron felt that he could allow this, could give himself up in this way.

He could, with Alicia, accept the stretched and meager thing of life, the little rush of youth and then the slow, vague drift of the rest, until the sidewards tug at the end, into something else, some fluorescent reward-world, perhaps, or just into the bizarre math of nothingness, the distant and sincere art of it—and if he could allow all this, if he could feel okay with all this, then, he guessed, so could Alicia and her parents, and his own parents. But he could not comprehend his parents or anyone else accepting things in this way, could not feel anything vicariously but fear, worry, and regret. And if his parents couldn't accept, if no one else could, then maybe he couldn't either. He knew he couldn't, actually, because though he understood, now, the possibility of such a feeling he did not feel it, and if ever he had felt fine and worriless and accepting in the past it was, he knew, a fleeting, delusional thing. He knew now—knew only—that, in the end, there would be urgency and difficultness, there would be the oncoming and increasingly complicated need to resolve, to be convinced—to be, finally, appreciative, of having once lived, of having at least happened in this sudden and terrific (or was it terrifying?) world.

Aaron went and held Alicia's hand. There was a helicopter somewhere, and they listened to it; some chopping, flapping noise that maybe was a bird, or a bug—a dragonfly or moth, flying close.

"I'm staying here," Alicia said. "I'm moving home. I just decided, I'm not going back to school or Florida."

Aaron thought about their two-year lease. He thought about moving back home, with his own parents. "I like it here," he said, and waited for Alicia to say something else, but she didn't. He thought about their plans for spring break, for right now—hadn't they made plans?

They went back to her house and ate fruit. They watched TV.

"My brother doesn't even know who I am anymore," Alicia said in bed. She was crying. "My sister's said things to him. They hate me. I deserve it. I'm so selfish. Why did I leave? I shouldn't have majored in

English. My sister could have gone to college too. She would've double majored in useful things. I wasn't thinking, ever! What was I even doing? I didn't think one thing in four years." She laughed a little, but it was mostly just crying, and she kept talking, and while she talked she moved—she shook a little; her chest, in fits—and Aaron, holding her, felt that moving, the turning of things inside, the loosening of it all, the press and shape of the bones in her back, all of which he was just faintly aware of, as he was thinking hard, thinking of something for both of them, something not to absolve what they were doing, but to absolve what the world was doing, what it *was*. And in this thinking, then—this incommunicable, impossible thinking; *why are there things?*—he began to feel a leaving, a vagueness and gravitylessness of self. And from some faraway place, now, from some else and momentary place, he became aware of a strange and bodiless squirming in his arms, a warm and pulsing thing, shifting against him in revisions—in increments and illusions—as he held, carefully, on, and began to fold and pack at himself, so that he might enter, finally, the experience of this thing, and staunch it, at its free and anonymous source, its phantom, nowhere heart that surely must be there; hidden, maybe, but real, and findable—if one wanted enough, and tried hard—as, if not, then where was one to go with all their white and toneless feelings? Where was one to take all their changed and used-up feelings of youth?

**Love is the Indifferent God
of the Religion in which
Universe is Church**

Sean had been spending his nights leisurely, with much intuition and very little actual engagement with the real world—the real world outside that was really happening. He was twenty-one. He lived with his older brother, Chris, in Manhattan, and dreamt mostly of love. These were terrible, cloying dreams. They involved prolonged moments of passion, vague and painted colors, and people sitting around in a sort of curtained and euphoric gloom, which was what love, in Sean's dreams, seemed to be. He slept in the daytime, on the sofa, and would wake, sometimes, with such an awful, spongy feeling of love—the soggy cake of it pressed against his heart like another heart—that he would then move through the apartment, the one long room of it, like a hallway gone wrong, in an unenlightened sort of searching (where was the beloved?), not touching anything, but just moving, between things (piles of clothes, the TV, the low white raft of his brother's bed), feeling husked and ancient and—sitting, then, back on the sofa—thankless, as what was there, in this cheap and witless world, to be thankful for? Not much, Sean knew. He didn't like the world, and the world had perhaps grown weary of him.

The world was weary of him!

Though probably it was not even love that Sean dreamed of, but some sleight of love, some trick of crush or inwardly thwarted desire, like a chemical seed; or else some boldly fraudulent expectation—an expectation that leads a fantasy out into the real world, gets it an apartment and, illegally, a job—as Sean had probably never been in love. He'd once told a girlfriend that he loved her, but had then felt suddenly vanquished, as if in swift and arrow-y battle, on some nighttime field; as if the world, in that moment, had thought of him, and mastered him; memorized and set him aside, like a learned thing. The world was maybe finished with Sean. And yet—he remained. Alive, doing things (eating, writing a novel, moving to Manhattan), as there was still, and always, the feeling—the suspicion—that the world knew him, and loved him, that the world was trying hard to convey this, was forming itself a language, progressing gradually, thoughtwardly, and slowly, along. Which was, perhaps, the sensation of being alive—the reason why Sean existed, kept going—the waiting of that, the faith in it, that there was a big thing of love out there, a mansion of it, and that the world, however incompetent, was trying every day to get Sean there, was thinking of where he should go, and how.

Sean woke up to Annie talking. "I've been having the suicide-note dream," Annie was saying. "I struggle with sentence structure, voice—is this me? is this my true voice?—I line edit, move the adverb around. I die finally of natural causes, which I deserve." Annie was sitting on the bed, facing Sean, who lay on the sofa, under blankets. Chris lay beside Annie, on his back. He had the *New Yorker*, which he held above him in an excruciating way.

"Oh," Annie said. "And sometimes I feel like my life's out there, in outer space—a spacecraft or moon— and any moment it's going to move down and smush me, all slow-motion-like." Annie kept very still for a few seconds. She's become jaded with herself, Sean thought tolerantly. "God," she said, "my head aches. It aches with both a love and a longing for the present, changing moment. I can feel it changing." She slapped a hand down behind her; it hit Chris's thigh. Annie was Chris's girlfriend.

"Massage me," Chris said. He tossed the *New Yorker* onto a pile of clothes on the floor. He rolled onto his side, toward the window, which overlooked 29th street. There were faraway siren sounds, the rush and voice of city noise, much like a beach shore—a beach shore, though, with cabs instead of waves, buildings instead of gulls. It was late evening, and summertime.

Annie was chopping at Chris's side. "Okay," Chris said. "Stop."

Sean closed his eyes to go back to sleep. He had been dreaming before, something watery and baffling. I want to learn, Sean thought. Swimming, he thought. Time swished and pocked inside of him, like a bowl of water with a fish in it that was also him. He wondered tentatively if he was asleep. He felt something on his legs. Annie had come over and sat on him. "I've got a sister," she said. "Want to meet her?"

Something inside of Sean's body, something small and squishy, shifted a little—a lymph node, perhaps.

"She's Maryanne," Annie said.

"Maryanne," Sean said. He felt the long bones of Annie's legs piling against his own.

"Annie," Chris said. He lay wrapped in his blanket on the floor, which was wood. Annie went to him. "Let's go to my place," she said. "To have incredible sex." Chris unwrapped himself and stood. "There's no such thing as incredible sex," he said. Annie beamed at him. She laughed. They went to Annie's place. Sean fell asleep. When he woke, he drank orange juice. He sat on the sofa in the dark. He was thinking about showering—the hard-tiled attack of it, the soap always slipping away like an unrequited, mocking love. The water would be never-ending. Unstoppable. To take a shower, it seemed a risky, harrowing thing. To build a fire, Sean thought. To build an enormous bonfire. Sean stood up. He lay on his brother's bed. Love, he thought. Maryanne, he was thinking. He felt wild and agitated. He didn't like this feeling—it was something of the past, twisting forward and back in knots—as he had recently, and for some time now, been a calmer person, someone with an unsentimental acceptance of things, a discerning and philosophic nature, no teenage angst, no vague desperation; because waking at night, Sean knew, was a changing thing. Each time, you craved less, you forgot a little of the shiny-loud world, the exploding appliance of faces in daytime—the dancing, thrashing equipment of things in the sun. You woke at night and something serene and foliaged gathered behind your eyes—a pale cache of forest—and, waking up, moving out from your mind, a part of you stayed there. In that dimmed place, some fragile, once-hurt part of you said, "What's this. This is nice. Okay then. Stay here then."

A few days later Chris came home early in the evening with Chinese food and woke up Sean, who had been dreaming of Maryanne.

"Broccoli and fried tofu," Chris said. "Extra mayonnaise and lettuce. I know you like that."

Sean went for the Chinese food. In his dream, he had been outside of himself. He was everything there was except for himself. He was all the pure and unpeopled love of the world. He was God, perhaps. He was also an eye. He saw himself and who he understood to be Maryanne, far below, lounging on a gaseous, Neptunish sort of field, lain rosy as shawls—shadowy and shifting as the insides of a thing.

"Let's rent a movie tonight," Chris said. "Mutant turtles. Your favorite. Splinter's Big Revenge."

Sean was eating the Chinese food. He was back in his dream, drifting through the outer-planet-y world of it, everything soft and purple and destroyed; unpulsing and beautiful as the bland, sweet skin of an eggplant. Was this love? Sean wondered. He put tofu in his mouth.

"I rented this already," Chris said. "No turtles for you." He was looking and grinning at Sean, who was staring down at the Chinese food. Chris tossed the movie on the sofa. Sean stared at the food, then moved—quite gracefully, he thought while doing it—to the movie and sat down beside it. "Can you put it in and rewind it?" Chris said. His voice could go high-pitched sometimes, a little beseeching, like a shy person's in a moment of extroversion, and it did now. "Sean, fast forward the previews?" Sean put his food down, picked up the movie. He remembered a noisy something from childhood, something brotherly and laughing, and felt the tiniest of sadnesses—the sadness of an ant, a mite, and a mosquito—stamping lightly against his heart, like a little rain.

There was a full-length mirror against the TV, and Chris, as he was moving it, now, dropped it. Sean saw on the floor a patch of glass, dark and unsparkling as leaves. Chris did not move for a few seconds; his eyes, Sean saw, were unfocused; his mouth unmoving and wet, imbedded in his head like a flat and creamy stone.

"It's just a mirror," Sean said.

Chris got a broom and swept the glass into a pile of clothes. He carried the broken mirror to his bed, then to the front door. "Don't worry so much," Sean said. "It's a mirror." Though he often caught himself assuming—wishing, probably—that everyone was the same, Sean knew that he and his brother (and everyone else) were hopelessly, and mysteriously, he felt, different. Chris set the mirror against the TV, back in its original place. The top half of it was intact, in a blade, like a guillotine. Sean felt anxious.

Chris went to his bed and lay on it, facing the window.

"Do you want to watch the movie?" Sean said.

Chris made a noise and sustained it. The noise got louder, then stopped.

Sean put the movie in. My brother deserves to be happy, he thought. What can happen in this world? he wondered nauseously. Can anything ever really happen? He looked at the sofa. He lay on it. The movie was not rewound. Sean watched the end credits and fell asleep.

"Next time I'll bring Maryanne here," Annie said to Sean. "What do you think?"

"Okay," Sean said. He lay under blankets on the sofa. Chris was in the shower; had been singing loudly, but had then stopped.

Annie was jumping, now, on the bed. "Sometimes I think I'm all these different people at once," she said while jumping. "Like five people. And they all want to use this same brain. And this brain's tired. This brain says, 'Four of you need to go,' and sometimes I start myself to go, because why should I get priority over these other four people?" Annie sat and smiled at Sean.

Sean tried to focus on his own life. "Have you seen *Annie Hall*?" he said. He had wanted to say something about his own life.

"No. But one time I dreamed I was Woody Allen," she said. "No one liked me anymore. People chased me in a hotel. Then I jumped out a window. I survived the fall, but there was a nail in my stomach. I walked a little and I thought, 'Well, I'll go make a movie now.'" Annie yawned very slowly and quietly. Her mouth opened wide. Sean looked at her teeth, the private collection of them, packed tightly inside of her small, elegant head, like a secret behind the face, a white and shocking hobby. It made Sean nervous. He felt perilous, then fleeting, and then a little excited.

"Woody Allen's *Annie Hall*," Annie said. "That's so sad. I mean, I don't know. Is it sad?"

Sean didn't remember what that movie was about. He remembered something about tennis, the hardness and slowness of tennis, the incapacitation of it, unmasterable as a bad dream, how the tennis ball would always soar from the racket—like a surface-to-air missile—over fences and walls. "Woody Hall," Sean said.

Annie laughed. "Annie Flame," she said. "That should be my pen name. I've written a novel." She stared at Sean. "Annie Flame would be my pen name and in interviews I'd take from a duffel bag a metal spike, one of those railroad ones. I'd say I was thinking of getting my forehead pierced. I'd hold the spike to my forehead, to demonstrate. I'd quote myself constantly. Myself and one other person. Einstein. That would be my career plan. In real life, I'd have this other persona—of sanity and love. It makes me sad, talking like this. I should stop."

Sean smiled pleasantly, quite naturally, which surprised and pleased him. "What's your novel called?"

"It's, 'Ten Digital Photographs of Eleven Tiny, Tortured Souls.'" Annie looked at Sean. "That's not what it's called," she said.

Chris came out of the bathroom in an audible thrust of steam, like an occult appearance—fully dressed. His face was wet. "Annie," he said. "I feel bad again today." Annie went to him and hugged him and they went out somewhere.

Sean moved from the sofa to the bed. I maneuvered deviously from the sofa to the bed, he thought. He was just a child, he knew. A little boy. He had written a novel, though. He, too, had written a novel. There were clams in the novel. A pile of them, on some lost and lightless seafloor; trembling, making whizzing noises, like straws, and then shooting apart, finally—exploding—

from the force of bemusement and lovelessness. The clams were symbolic somehow; they had to have been. Or had they? It was a desperate, unfun novel—very strange, told with an incomprehensible sort of irony. It had real people also, not just clams. Sean had spent a year on it—a year, he now realized, that he remembered nothing about. Try harder to remember your own life from now on, Sean thought, and then fell into a dreamless sleep. When he woke, he went immediately and took a shower. He walked out into the night, thinking languageless thoughts. He felt new and released—newly released, like some rare and squinting animal; a flying wombat or African wild ass. His eyes felt complex and weightless inside his head. He ran suddenly across a street. At night, he knew, there could be the belief that something never before felt might be felt, something new. You could allow yourself quite easily this view of the world—this thrilling, midnightly faith—of there being something out there that loved you, that, at night, worshipped and searched for you, like a past life seeking its next, wanting desperately the continuation of itself. And though it would probably never find you, it would also, you believed at night, never give up, and this was enough—that something was out there and desperate and on its way. This was less in the city, though. In the city, it was mostly just too loud. There were too many buses. Sean went to a sushi place on St. Marks. He had miso soup, and ice water. Maryanne, he thought. Who is Maryanne? He looked across the restaurant at his waitress—a dark and neighborly thing, sort of ominous—and thought, I am in love with that person; then went home and dreamt the discolored dream of being in love with someone who did not exist. He woke and did not stop himself (Maryanne, he thought, Maryanne, Maryanne) as there was a worldless sort of desire—a faithless, gaping, windstorm-y thing—that could swell in you as you had to end one day and move into the next; and to relieve this, the indestructible hole of it, you made severe and alarming promises of nothing and everything; you built elaborate thoughts, like houses—mansions, other worlds—and you moved, wrenchingly, stupidly, in; not knowing, feeling, or believing anything, except that you had arrived, made it to some sort of love, some vaporization of love, like a cream of water, perhaps, but a love nonetheless, in this vast and lacerated place inside your head, inside your thoughts, and so could, finally, then, sleep.

In the apartment Sean had music on very loud. This was despairing guitar music from the mid 90's. Chris had gone somewhere with Annie for the week. It was 3 a.m.,

TAO LIN

and Sean was cleaning—going around with a trash bag, stuffing things in; humming harmonies and sometimes singing.

In the morning, Sean went for Chinese takeout. Back home, he put on despairing acoustic music. He ate, poured juice. The music was very good. Sean stopped for a moment and held himself very still. This is good, he thought. I'm being serious, he thought. "I am extremely happy," he said aloud. He put his food down. He jumped on his brother's bed. He lay down. He wanted to laugh or something. Love, he thought. He got up, turned off the music. He watched TV. He went to sleep.

It was dark out when Sean woke. He put on music, washed the dishes. He wiped the TV and the desk with wet paper towels, and the floor. He showered with the door open, the music loud. He went out for coffee. He stopped at a bookstore and got a job application. Outside, crossing Fifth Avenue, he looked up at the buildings and felt a kind of rapture, something of apology and thanks and intelligence—though maybe just a thing of coffee and wakefulness—forming, like a good idea (the world thinking hard, finally), here, in the little wind, the slightly infrared space between the buildings, the wet, shucked gemstars of the traffic lights, and all the glassy windows above, bright and comprehending as

eyes, watchful as a world that wanted, truly, to know—
and to love—all its lost and bewildered people.

Sean woke on his brother's bed. "Sean," Annie said. She
and Chris were back. "Come with us to see a block-
buster Hollywood movie." Her hair was dyed an incon-
sistent green, like a fern plant.

"Maryanne wants to meet you for a blind date,"
Annie said in the movie theatre. She sat between Sean
and Chris, leaned against Chris and looking at Sean.
"Maryanne. Isn't that a pretty name?"

"Maryanne, who is Maryanne," Chris said.

"I like that name," Sean said. He was thinking of a
dream he had, a few days ago, in which love was a
skeleton that hovered through the night; just one skeleton for all the world—a logistical mistake, Sean understood in his dream—gliding toe-swept over oceans,
under bridges, through walls; the bones and ghost of it
entering and leaving bedrooms at night, like a wantless
thief; a clean, dead thing with the temperament of a
cloud. The dream had gone on and on and was sooth-
ing in a chalky, religious way, like a sourceless and messageless yet somehow affecting prayer. Now, though, the
whole thing seemed just irritating. The skeleton, Sean
now felt, was not love, but some failed manifestation of

love—high-flying and loud, jangling its bones, chomping its jaws in a false and godless laughter.

"Maryanne was dropped on her head as a small girl," Annie was saying. "But instead of making her brain-damaged, it made her think beautifully and oddly. She was knocked sideways on the IQ scale, not downwards."

"How come?" Sean said. He had spent the rest of last week renting low-budget, existential films, drinking beer and coffee, gazing somehow nostalgically from across the room at the bookstore job application—kind of depressed.

"How old is your sister?" Chris said.

Annie sat up very straight. "My sister," she said. "She isn't restrained by time or space. She's not like that. I don't know. She's not a robot. This isn't science fiction masterpiece theatre." Annie paused. "I could say she's ten or twenty but that wouldn't be true. She's just *there*. She's not even a sister, really." Annie laughed. She stood up. "Hey, wow," she said. "There's Maryanne." She pointed at a girl sitting alone in the front row. "Sean, go sit by her. She's lonely. Maybe a little hope-less, sitting in the front row. But look at her hair. She's fixed it up, shampooed it."

"I don't know Maryanne," Sean said.

"Where's Maryanne?" Chris said without moving. "Thanks, Sean. For cleaning the apartment."

"Maryanne," Annie shouted. Some people, not the girl, turned around. "Go before the movie starts. Just point up here for confirmation, I'll be waving."

"No," Sean said. Annie pulled him up. Sean looked around. The world seemed strange, but then it wasn't strange anymore, it was just the world. "Okay," he said. "But come with me." He would go, he thought. He would get himself inescapably in love, like a good trouble; love would stare blankly at him, he would not flinch, and love, then, would murder him, drag him to a gray, underground place, freeze his corpse, and, over time, eat him. Annie pushed Sean into the aisle. She sat back down. Sean felt tall and dizzy. He went carefully down the steps. At the front row, he smiled at the girl, said something, and pointed back up at Annie, who was standing and waving. The girl stood up. Her face was startled and afraid. She was middle-aged. She touched her hair and sat down. Sean was looking, now, at the floor, and it seemed to Annie like he had fallen asleep, standing there. The lights went off.

Sean came back up and sat down. There was a small pounding at the back of his head, a tapping against the inside-back of his skull—the brain bored with itself;

wanting out, perhaps, drilling slowly, wearily, at the bone.

"Don't worry, Sean," Annie whispered. She looked at him. She patted his thigh.

"Good one," Sean whispered to her. It really was good, he thought.

Later, during the movie, Annie whispered in Sean's ear, "That's what you have to do. Pretend you know these people. Pretend they love you. They *can* love you. Think about it." The movie was about James Bond, who had a speedboat that could, if the situation called for it, which it did—twice—fit in the palm of his hand. He was a very busy man, too busy for love—except for a terse, witty, hyper-sexy sort of love.

After the movie, they went for sushi. "Still believe I have a sister named Maryanne?" Annie said. "Think I'm making that up?"

"Maybe," Sean said.

"I do," Annie said. "She has the cataractous gaze of a child prodigy entering into a scorched land. One time she tossed an ice cream cone underhand into a third-floor window. The cold thing went without a sound into that hard, brick building. It was like a little epiphany of the physical world."

"I like that," Sean said.

"Annie. Listen to yourself," Chris said. He stood up. "What are you doing right now?" He adjusted his pants and sat down. He had a look on his face, Sean saw, like he might scream in such a horrifyingly quiet, mutated, and frequencyless way that the rules of the universe would then have to be changed.

"You're in a bad mood," Annie said. She hugged Chris. She looked at him. "I love you," she said.

"I didn't mean to say that," Chris said uncertainly. He looked away, loudly said, "I'm joking," then looked back and began to talk about whether or not it was a crime against humanity to buy coffee from Starbucks. It was a public company, so was driven by profit, would create a greater divide between the rich and the poor. But people were maybe better able to fall in love inside of Starbucks, with those plush sofas. But were people supposed to love other people, themselves, the entire world, or love itself? Chris looked around. He said that he hadn't been thinking about any of this until now; he'd been thinking about chess—how bizarre and depressing it was—and then was somehow all of a sudden talking about Starbucks. He said he felt a lot better now—maybe. He wasn't sure. He spread his fingers on his head and began to massage it. Annie peeled Chris's hands off, replaced those hands with her own, quoted Einstein ("Only a life lived for others is worthwhile") and then said something about learning to love, how it was a kind of memorization, a set of facts to place in your mind, a kind of future memory— a framework—to move into. Sean was trying to listen, to figure that out, when he got up—unconsciously, he thought while doing it—to use the bathroom. He washed his hands. Maryanne, he thought. He made a smile at the mirror above the sink. He made an angry face, a neutral face. He moved his head very close to the glass—the tricky, world-in-world depth of it, like a wise and airy ice. He could fall in, he knew, into the higher intelligence of the mirror, the keen and confident indifference of it, how it continuously took you in and doubted you and reflected your doubted self back into the world. Sean stared at his face. Where did he come from? What must one believe in? Where did love come from? He felt that these were three very legitimate questions.

In the morning Annie came over with a little girl. Sean hadn't slept yet and was about to. Chris was watching TV. "Is your crab-cake recipe better than love?" the TV was saying. "Better than, um, sex?"

"Hi, small girl," Chris said.

"This is Maryanne," Annie said. The girl looked about five or six. She held onto a corner of Annie's dress, which was layered red and white—she had on two dresses.

"Who's Maryanne?" the little girl whispered. Her hand was very tiny.

"You're Michelle," Annie said to the little girl. "Most of what I said was not true," Annie said to Chris and Sean. "Of course the truth is like a box of 56 crayons." She paused. "Goddamn," she said in a kind tone. "It's okay to say goddamn around Michelle."

The little girl wandered over to Sean.

"Hi, Maryanne," Sean said.

"Michelle," said the little girl.

"I forgot," Sean said.

"Hi," Michelle whispered. She moved very close to Sean. "Do you have a pet?"

Sean scooted away from Michelle then back to where he just was. He shook his head. Something was scrolling across the cramped sky of his mind, a white and messageless banner, folding across itself.

Michelle took something out of her pocket. A lima bean. She held it close to her chest and petted it while looking at Sean. Her eyes seemed flawless in a cut and auctionable way—a bit outlandish, Sean thought critically. He stared at her.

"That's her pet bean," Annie said. "She says it's a dog. Michelle, share what's its name."

Michelle put the bean in her pocket and stepped back, away from Annie. "Let me do it myself," Michelle said. Her face turned red. She held Sean's hand and glared at Annie.

Sean looked at Chris, who was staring at the TV, which became very loud suddenly—"For the last twenty years I loved someone who loved someone else, who was not a thing of the human species, but a major S&P 500 corporation. So I just collapsed and fell on the bed. The bed was not a *water*bed. It was park bench."

Sean made an effort to wish the world well, but then accidentally gave it—he felt this with clarity—a damning curse. He thought of maybe lying down. He was very sleepy. The little girl is holding my hand, he thought. He lost track of things for a moment, and then time seemed to pass blunderingly, suddenly, by, in a flapping bunch, like an unclogged flock of something. Sean was taken aback. Time had certain obligations, he knew.

"I'm hungry," Chris said. He stood up. "I want the salad. The Japanese place. St. Marks." They left for the restaurant, the same one as the night before. After eating, they stood outside. They looked at the sky. It was cloudy and a little pink. There was nothing to say about it. Annie bought ice cream. Sean wandered into a deli and came out with a coffee whose largeness seemed highly creative.

On Fifth Avenue, Annie ran ahead. She bent at her knees and jumped a little. Her ice cream cone floated up into the air, brushed against a closed second-floor window, fell on the sidewalk. Annie's mouth moved in something like a laugh—Chris, Sean, and Michelle saw—and she ran into a store and came back out when everyone else had caught up.

"What is wrong with you," Chris said. His voice was neutral and disconnected, more sound than language. Sean mimicked his brother aloud—"What is wrong with you"—and laughed. Chris looked at him.

"What is wrong with you," Chris said again.

Sean laughed again.

"I'm helping you," Annie was saying to Chris. "Doing strange things will help you. Didn't you like that?" She hugged Chris. She looked at him.

"Sorry," Chris said.

"You seem happy," she said.

"No," Chris said. "I mean—maybe." He pointed weakly at something across the street. Sean thought of clams and laughed. Chris looked at him.

Back at the apartment, Michelle had been in the bathroom for a long time. Sean—on the sofa—finished his coffee, put the cup on the table, and felt a vague desire for the cup. I'm a red cup, said the cup. Sean picked it up, set it back. The cup was huge. Sean grinned. Annie and Chris were on the bed. "We're sitting here waiting for Michelle," Annie said. "We're not doing nothing, we're doing something." They could hear Michelle in the bathroom, talking in hushed, secretive tones.

"What's my job?" Chris said slowly. "I forgot how I make money. Oh. Never mind."

Michelle came out and whispered something in Annie's ear. Annie went to Chris's desk and swept all the stuff there—all the useless crap, Sean thought instantaneously—to one side.

Michelle took her bean out of her pocket, and then a little bed, which was toilet paper inside of a sushi soy-sauce holder. She stole that from the Japanese restaurant, Sean thought enthusiastically. Michelle put the bed on the table, the bean on the bed. She covered exactly half the bean with toilet paper.

They were all watching her do this. "Stop it," Michelle said. She moved her body so that it blocked what she was doing.

Chris turned on the TV—a dating show.

"The bean—the *dog* is treated so well," Annie said. "That's no good. Without pain, pleasure is an unsatisfying, irritating thing. With pain... it's an urgent, leaving thing. Is that too pessimistic? Michelle?"

Michelle ignored Annie in a way that was visible on her face. She crawled to the middle of the bed and curled atop a blanket, which Sean had earlier folded very neatly into a square. On the sofa, Sean felt that his posture was very straight. "I feel good," he said aloud. He felt very awake.

Annie picked up Michelle by picking up the blanket she lay on. Michelle's face turned red and she scrunched her eyes very tight. Annie set Michelle and the blanket on a corner of the bed and then lay down. "Christopher," she said. Chris turned off the TV. They went to sleep. It had gotten dark outside. Sean stood at a distance and looked at Chris, Annie, and Michelle. They all lay very still. They seemed to be pretending somehow. We're not a part of your reality, they said. Look at how good I am, said the bed. Useful. Yeah, Sean thought. He looked at them for a very long time and went into an exquisite sort of daze. He felt enlightened and spearminty as gum. He went outside, walked around, bought coffee, came back, sat on the sofa. He felt like he'd hopped out and instantly hopped back in, with coffee. He watched TV on mute. He drank coffee. The TV was showing a movie and Sean found it extremely amusing and impressive. The second the movie ended, Chris woke up and said in an annoyed tone of voice that he wanted to go to the same Japanese place again. It was after midnight. Michelle took the bean out of its bed and went into the bathroom. "Be careful," she said from inside. Her voice was sleepy and loud. "Please. Good. I love you. That's love." Michelle came out. She stood by the door, and began to blush.

"The bean uses the bathroom," Annie said.

"No, stop, you don't even know," Michelle screamed. She faced away from Annie. She went back in the bathroom, came out, punched Annie's thigh. They all left for the restaurant.

By Union Square, a strange man asked Annie to take his picture.

The man was strange, Sean knew, because he had on a shirt that said, "Love, Italian Style."

Annie took the man's camera and gave it to Michelle. The man looked worried. "Hold it," he said. He had another camera in hand, a larger one. "Thanks so much," he said, and moved forward, grinning. Michelle snapped a picture with flash. There was a second man, now, who was squinting at Sean from a very close distance. Sean noticed that he was staring straight through this man.

"Let her," Annie told the man. But he had taken back the camera and entered a store. He and the second man stood inside, behind glass. One of them was pointing at Michelle. There seemed to be four of them now—

four men, each one strange in his own unique way. Sean did not understand. He laughed suddenly. The novel had clams, he thought. He laughed again.

"Do you want a camera for Christmas?" Annie asked Michelle. "Photographers are well-respected and artfully political. Artfully political," she said carefully.

"I want a horse-drawn carriage for Christmas," Chris said. "To run myself over with. Just kidding."

"I want us all to live together in a house somewhere, not doing anything." Annie said. She looked at Michelle. "A ginger-bread house. What do you want Sean?"

I want to be in love and out of this place, Sean thought immediately, and then felt the nausea of that thought, the massive, animal flu of it. He didn't want anything, ever, he thought extravagantly. Actually, he knew exactly what he wanted. He had thought about this before—last week when he was kind of depressed. He wanted to enter into himself, sit inside his own body, and look out from there, to see what he would do. He wanted to continue doing things, but wanted just to watch that happening, and not actually do anything. "I want—" Sean said.

"He took my picture!" Michelle screamed. She began to climb Sean, who watched her noncommittally, then picked her up, cradling her legs and upper back.

"Michelle's the smartest in her class," Annie said. "Her teachers are all useless. All teachers are all useless. Where's Chris?"

Chris was walking toward the restaurant. Annie ran to him. Sean, carrying Michelle, stared at Annie running, then began to jog in her direction.

"You're bumpy," Michelle said. Sean looked down and saw that Michelle's eyes were wide-open and calm, which made him feel happy. "You're not good at being smooth," Michelle said. Chris was ahead, going very fast, and Sean began to run, to keep up. He concentrated on rolling his feet, letting the heel land first. He felt that he might fall and dent his forehead; or else very quickly descend into the concrete, like stairs.

At the restaurant they sat at the sushi bar. They sat Chris, Sean, Michelle, Annie. Chris ordered three house salads, which were rushed out immediately in a sort of prolonged tic on the part of the waitress. "Sorry," said the waitress. She smiled directly at Sean. How many times had Sean been here in this one very long day? He counted in his head. One, two, three. Sean smiled back at the waitress. Little did she know, Sean thought, the life he lived—it was less a life than a museum and a church of life. A repository of things clubbed-on-the-head, stuffed, put on display, worshipped from behind glass. This was a place impossible for romance, a place where tea was brewed, earnestly, from paint chips, glass shards, and small change. In this world, Sean knew, one could put faith in a toe bone, a blood bone, a cartilage of eye—all the unloved contributors of one's own body-world. Though, what was a blood bone? Were there, perhaps, bones in the blood? Tiny ones that swam? Skeletons of some lost and wayless plasma-people? What about clams? None of this, Sean thought very carefully and slowly, was true, of course. He made an effort to concentrate on the real world—the actual place outside where real things happened every day, supposedly.

Annie was hugging Chris and asking about his salads and Chris was unresponsive.

Then Annie was back in her seat saying to Michelle, "Your eyebrows are going to grow muscles if you keep looking that way. Do you want big eyebrow muscles on your face? It's okay if you do. You can do anything you want." Annie took something from her pocket and put it in her mouth. She did that twice. "You're a very privileged young girl," she said. "Would you like horse-riding lessons? Would you like to eat exuberant salads, with variegated wild nuts? That can be arranged." Annie was looking at her hands, which were clasped in front of her. "Your life is ahead of you and it's crazy. A jumping, darting thing. A winged-frog thing, being dart-gunned. Do you want to be a quiet girl or a loud girl? Happily sad or sadly happy? Who will you love? For what reasons? Would you like piano lessons or violin?" Annie turned slowly, at the neck, toward Michelle. "It's not too late to be a concert pianist. It's not too late to believe in a loving God."

"Stop," Michelle whispered. "Stop doing that," she shouted.

"You didn't mean to whisper," Annie said. "So cute."

Michelle pushed Annie, who leaned into the push, canceling it.

"Just, stop, please," Chris murmured. "Bad..."

"I don't love you," Michelle said to Annie.

Sean had been thinking about one time, a long time ago in Florida, when Chris had chased him down and tied his arms behind his back with a belt, his legs together with shoelaces, and then sprayed him with the water hose. Sean couldn't stop laughing, even while being sprayed in the face; it was in the front yard, on the grass, and Sean had later pulled the hose, taut, into the living room and sprayed his brother, Chris, who had been eating a plate of microwaved nuggets. Actually, Sean hadn't done that, but he was imagining it now— skylight, sliding glass door, chicken nuggets—without taking into consideration if it had really happened.

He was imagining this and smiling and staring at Annie, and then Annie was smiling back at him and they smiled at each other for a very long time, nothing else happening in the world.

Then Sean was yawning and blinking a very slow blink. He noticed that he was staring at something not Annie. His eyes weren't focusing. Focus, Sean told his eyes. He exerted willpower at his eyes. There was a fork. I'm used for eating, said the fork. Throw it, Sean thought. He wanted to have fun. He touched his mouth and felt that he was still smiling. Good, he thought. He yawned and put some of his fingers in the hole of his mouth. He wouldn't ever sleep again, he thought promisingly, never again. Clams, he thought. He saw that Chris was pointing his finger, ordering appetizers off the menu. All of them, Sean thought, give him all the appetizers. The waitress had her notepad. Sean couldn't decipher her face. He felt that he knew her intimately. She had a pen and a notepad and then she was leaving. "Beer," Chris shouted. "Saki."

"Oh, wow," Annie said. "Maryanne has the same consonant-vowel configuration as Michelle. I guess that isn't very interesting." Michelle stood and began to attack Annie. She kicked Annie. She hit Annie with a spoon. Annie had a worried look on her face. "Oh, Michelle," she said. "Hit me, please. I'm sorry. I don't

154   TAO LIN

know what to do. I really don't. How do I help us? You and Chris. You and Sean and Chris."

Sean looked at his brother, who seemed to be weeping, very quietly and strangely, his face down, almost touching his salad bowls. Sean wanted to spray him with the hose. He wanted badly to do that ten years ago. I'll do it, Sean thought. The logic of this blanked his mind. Then Michelle was holding his hand, leading him someplace, and now they stood outside the restaurant, looking in through glass.

Annie was hugging Chris at the sushi bar. She turned and looked for Michelle and Sean and saw them standing outside, holding hands. The precocious child, her daughter—how she loved her little Michelle—was staring right at her, fiercely but sleepily; her eyes a bit unfocused. Sean, the young boy, was yawning. He had the admonished, ever-surrendering face—the wet eyes— of someone who would only ever love from a distance, in secret, a kind of nauseous, searching half-love, a love dizzied by its own halfness, made faithful by its own dizziness. He was yawning again. He hadn't slept, Annie knew.

Michelle led Sean inside. She walked slowly around, holding Sean's hand. Sean gazed at people with a keen and intensifying indifference. He experienced a distinct moment of nonexistence, and then became aware that he was staring at teriyaki. Who are you? Sean thought. The meat rolled over. It was chicken. It had a sad, slick sauce on it—a savvy dressing that it maybe, Sean thought cautiously, did not want. But it needed that sauce. It wanted to be eaten. Michelle was asking a stranger where the bathroom was. Then Sean opened the bathroom door and Michelle pushed him inside. She went inside. The bathroom was small and dark and Sean turned on the light. "No," Michelle said. Sean turned off the light. He stared into the darkness. Love, he thought. He was yawning. People outside were laughing. The sound was distorted. "I left my salmon at your house," someone said excitedly. Cold air was moving down from above and Michelle was talking loudly. "She threw sand at my pet dog. It was Bean. She says things on purpose because she's an annoying mommy…" I do not know what she is talking about, Sean thought very slowly. Michelle was crying softly, then very loudly. Sean felt that he was somewhere else, a place where he was yet somewhere else. Thanks, Sean thought. Thank you, world. Something inside of him was grabbing at air. Something else was on its way, was moving, steady and brainward, like an inchoate thought, something forming and loving and true—but it was a tiny thing, a distant and tired thing, and it was slowing, giving up, maybe turning around. Michelle was crying and saying, "I don't even love any real person..." and someone was knocking at the door, from below. It was Chris. "Sean," he said. "Maryanne." He kicked the door again, then had the sudden and engrossing thought that tomorrow, and every day after, he might wake up feeling exactly the same as he did right now, which made his body shake a little. No one noticed that, though. No one was looking at Chris. Everyone was looking at the green-haired, red-and-white dressed girl, who was standing next to Chris, and who was saying, "People are staring, Michelle, Sean, right at me, as I'm saying these words they're staring at my mouth and inside of my mouth and now their faces are changing—as I'm talking, Chris, their faces are changing and changing..." Her voice was loud, but trembling, as if she were going to cry.

Cull the Steel Heart,
Melt the Ice one,
Love the Weak Thing;
Say Nothing of Consolation,
but Irrelevance, Disaster,
and Nonexistence; Have no
Hope or Hate—Nothing; Ruin
Yourself Exclusively,
Completely, and
Whenever Possible

Snow was everywhere that Friday, in clumps and hills, glassy and metastasized as SUVs, and none of it white. The sky was a bright and affected gray—lit from some unseen light source, and not really that interesting. People went up and down Sixth Avenue with the word *motherfucker* in their heads. They felt no emotions, had no sensation of life, love, or the pursuit of happiness, but only the knowledge of being stuck between a Thursday and a Saturday, air and things, this thought and the next, philosophy and action; birth, death, God, the devil, heaven, and hell. There was no escape, ever, was what people felt.

Colin himself was dressed lightly, in dark and enveloping colors. He felt of the same endless machinery and danceless, starless trance of the city at night, if a bit cold. He stood on the perimeter of Washington Square Park, waiting for Dana. They were going to a Leftover Crack show. Leftover Crack was a ska-punk band fronted by a person named Stza; their recent CD was "Fuck World Trade," Colin knew, as he owned that CD.

Dana crossed the street quickly, as if over water. She wore a yellow beanie, stood with Colin on the sidewalk. They smiled at each other and nothing else happened. The atmosphere was not conducive to talking. Visibility was low because of a fog. In the distance, vague things were falling or rising between the buildings. Bats, flying trash. Werewolves, throwing themselves off of roofs. Dana was holding herself with her own arms, Colin could see. They'd known each other almost four years, beginning with the first college-orientation thing before September 11th, but hadn't really talked in more than three. A few days ago they'd met on the street and made plans. Tonight, Dana's boyfriend was at a boxing seminar or something, was unavailable, so here she was with Colin.

In the street, a car idled by, a little off-kilter and without its lights on. An unmanned car, lost in the world. It spun slowly around and continued down the street, backwards and twisting.

It began to snow.

"Sure you want to do this?" Dana finally said.

Colin felt cold. He probably should've worn more clothing. The show was in Brooklyn, he knew, and they were in Manhattan. "Um," he said.

"I want to do something with you still," Dana said.

Colin looked at her. His eyes were very dry. He could feel his contact lenses there, little walls in front of his eyes. He yawned and Dana went out of focus, a bit wild and diagonal in the air, as if about to travel through time. There was snow on her beanie. Colin brushed at it. But it was just white dots—smiley faces.

"There was this beanie floating through the air the other day," Dana said. "Minding its own business, and I reached over and plucked it out. Like a flower or something. Not this one I'm wearing now. A different one. This really shitty one." She smiled, then laughed. "I never say 'shitty.' I've just been listening to this song. It goes, '*the world's a shitty place / I can't wait to die,*' and at the end he goes, '*just kidding world / you know I love you.*'"

Colin knew that song. There was nothing to say about it. "They should have beanies with beans on it, not smiley faces," he said.

"Yeah. Anything but smiley faces."

"When I see a smiley face I feel demented."

"What if beans were alive and they all had smiley faces," Dana said.

They talked some more like that. Dana seemed to move closer over time, then began to touch Colin's shoulder sometimes. Colin didn't know if this was flirting or what. He knew he didn't know anything about motivation, the world, the future, the past, or human beings. He knew that Dana was marrying her boyfriend. Actually, he did know many things. But it was maybe too many, and he didn't care. His knowledge was an indestructible machine, made of a million pieces of metal, and flying—a gigantic, gleaming, peripheral blur that Colin was not at all curious about.

A while ago, one night, Colin had eaten the universe, and from then on had felt black and spacey inside, had felt his heart, tiny and untwinkling, in some faraway center, white and tepid as a dot of Styrofoam.

Dana had changed her mind. She wanted now to see Leftover Crack. Would not do anything else, no matter what.

"I'm doing a film," she shouted on the train. "I'm filming tomorrow. Want to be in it?"

Colin said, "What did you just say?" Then realized what she had said. Then the train started screeching and someone began to play a saxophone. Colin told himself to ask Dana about the film later. There was a building that was Colin's future, a tall and glassy place that he'd have to enter, and if he didn't fill it, he'd end up wandering the floors, wheeling around on an office chair, rolling his own body on the carpet, like a log. But then probably that'd be a lot easier. Him in his empty building. Harmless, mute. Irrelevant.

Dana shouted something but Colin couldn't hear. He saw her mouth move in a laugh. "I'm going in there with white and green," a little girl screamed, "and you're going to choose green!" Dana took a paper from her pocket, gave it to Colin. A drawing of two whales; one with a fishhook in its mouth, a harpoon in its eye; the other with lipstick, squares for eyes—the saddest-looking whale Colin had ever seen—and a thought bubble:

I wish I could round these eyes
I don't like myself but I think I like you
Give me a kiss and shred off my face
Give me a very square farewell look

Colin read it and nodded at Dana. She was blushing. She touched her face, grinned, shouted something, took back her paper. They got off the train in Red Hook, Brooklyn. It was very quiet here. Snow had come down from heaven, swirled about, absorbed all the smoke and dust—all the coppery, spray painted wooziness of a city—and then fallen, thwarted, to the black and coagulated ground, stopped on its way to hell. There was not a deli anywhere, and no buses. A police van was ahead.

"Show's over," a policeman in the van said. "Concert's canceled." Colin and Dana kept walking toward the venue, a bit quicker. "Turn around and go home," the policeman said. "There's nothing here for you two."

Colin and Dana turned slowly around.

"Just kidding!" the policeman said. "Hey!"

As Colin and Dana walked by, the policeman smiled at Colin. Because of snow, they had to walk within touching distance of the van. All the cops inside, Colin saw, were distinctly different in body size. Maybe a dozen cops, all in jackets. "Have fun," the policeman said.

The venue was Polish-owned, had an outside area where kids smoked and where three Polish women—a mom, her daughters—sold hot dogs, vegetarian hot dogs, chips, and an orange, potion-y drink, which was in a large punch bowl. A hundred or so kids were out here.

Colin thought of saying something. He hadn't for a while. But he felt very calm, and a little dizzy; felt as if washed out by some sweet and anesthetic water, as he often did. Kids were moving in and out of shadows, being loud or elusive, eating chips or smoking. They were sad and pretty in their anguished and demonic colors, their piercings, their hands in their pockets. The bassist for Leftover Crack, Colin recognized, stood alone, eating a hot dog that was not vegetarian, drinking the orange drink.

Dana was looking at Colin. "I'm taking a vampire class," she said. "We just watch vampire movies."

Something black and warped was rippling through Colin's head, little voids, and he couldn't concentrate. Probably it was unacceptable to be distracted in this way, he knew, by nothing—by nothingness. It took him a minute or two to respond. "Is Bram Stoker a vampire?" he finally said.

"Bram Stoker," Dana said. "Are *you* a vampire?"

"Yes," Colin said. Leftover Crack's bassist was looking down into his orange drink. "I was a cat when I was five, for Halloween. With a cape." A cat from three to eleven, then a boy with a ghoul mask, then nothing. Halloween quickly became mostly for vandalism; no one dressed up anymore, just destroyed property, attacked one another openly and in teams. It was a different world back then. There were a thousand different worlds in the world, Colin knew. Each had a hundred thousand secrets locked-up in invisible steel rooms in the bright blue sky. Before bedtime, each night, you took a multiple-choice test based on those secrets. You never knew if you failed or what, and each morning you woke with the uncertainty of that. You also woke with a craving for new and requited love. The craving was unrelated to the uncertainty. Both were loyal only to their own causes. You yourself had no cause and seemed, at times, to be simply the effect of something. Fixed, unstoppable. Existing by momentum only, but pretending always otherwise.

"That's good for five," Dana said. She touched his elbow. "Colin, you were a vampire cat."

"Look at the bassist." Colin extended his arm straight out and pointed, startling himself in a dull and private way—he hadn't meant to point like this. Some kids saw Colin pointing and looked. The bassist noticed and moved the hot dog down to his side, held it there like it wasn't a hot dog, but something insurgent—a microphone or pipe bomb.

Dana laughed. "You're embarrassing him!"

She slowly pulled Colin's hand down.

"There aren't enough songs against McDonald's," Colin said. "There should be a song called 'Fuck

McDonald's.'" He felt suddenly excited, and looked directly into Dana's face. He was not afraid. There was her face. At night, it would move through his vision, colorless and behind the eyes, like a phantom, floating bird—a hood of wings, folding away. "Do you think McDonald's is objectively bad?"

"I think so," Dana said. "Yeah; I agree with you."

Colin looked away. Leftover Crack, he knew, had a song called "Fuck America"—it had begun to play in his head. It was catchy. It had rhyming couplets.

McDonald's will bloom as the major competition
Between Jesus and the Devil for this government's
   religion
People so caught up in the freedom that they see
While America's fucking over every single country

Something Something Chorus Something

Fuck America
Fuck America
Fuck America
Fuck America

(Outro)

Dana was talking about if she were Bill Gates. "I'd do things about McDonald's," she was saying. "I'd end the McDonald's corporation somehow. With Windows software."

"They'll sue you." Colin didn't feel excited anymore. He felt drugged and indifferent. Something enormous and depressed and on drugs had moved through him; had been watching him, from a distance, and had now come and moved through him.

"I'll sell them faulty windows that would keep breaking," Dana said. She laughed. "So their restaurants will look all dilapidated. When they sue me I'll bribe the Supreme Court. I'll give them supercomputers. Colin, I really like supercomputers for some reason. They're so big and sad. I just want to take care of them. I get these urges…"

Colin wondered if Dana talked this way to her boyfriend. He knew nothing about Dana's boyfriend. Except that his name was Tyson, and all Colin could ever think was Mike Tyson. Colin liked Mike Tyson. He didn't know much about Dana anymore. They had talked a lot at first, years ago, that first August before school, before September 11th—all day, walking up and down Manhattan, side to side, through parks—

but Colin couldn't remember any specifics unless he tried very hard, and he didn't feel like trying that hard.

Leftover Crack had a history of inter-band disputes. At a show Colin had attended, the guitarist had left the venue after Stza became depressed and smashed his guitar—the body snapping cleanly and quietly from the neck, as if willingly—and sang a few songs lying flat on his back. Another time, at CBGB, a few months after September 11th, the guitarist had on a fawn-colored sweater over a crisp white shirt for some reason and had said, in a sincere way, that he was proud to be an American, that it really moved him how everyone had come together. Then Stza had said that September 11th was the greatest day of his miserable life. Then they had played "Stop the Insanity (Lets End Humanity)," or something.

On stage now, Leftover Crack's bassist walked to his bass, picked it up, strapped it on, and stood waiting for the others. His face was expressionless and he did not move his eyes, mouth, head, or legs. His shirt said "NO-CA$H." The guitarist was asking the crowd for beer. Someone passed up a shiny blue plastic cup, but it wasn't beer.

"Somebody pass this fucker a beer," Stza said.

"If I don't get a beer," the guitarist said. "I'll put my guitar down, smoke some crack, drink a forty. Seriously, I don't care." He had just done a set with his own band; he had his own band.

"We all know, dude," Stza said. "We all know."

They played "Gay Rude Boys Unite (Take Back the Dance Hall)," their anti-homophobia song, "Money," their anti-money song, "Life is Pain," their anti-breeding song, and "Suicide (A Better Way)," their pro-suicide song. Behind them, against the wall, was a large upside-down American flag with a pentagram drawn over it in black marker. In the corner was a little silvery "666."

Colin and Dana stood to the side, back a little. Both had toilet paper packed in their ears. About ten songs in, Dana pushed Colin toward the middle and front. They were squished, were pushing forward and screaming the lyrics, and then Colin fell back into a circle-pit area, was okay for a while, moving quick and unharmed, but then was elbowed some place and smacked in the side by someone's fat, hard body. He fell to the ground, which was cool and sticky. Kids picked him up, righted him, squared his shoulders. "My shoe," Colin said. "My shoe fell off." Kids began to search for his shoe. Then someone was slapping Colin's cheek with his shoe and giving him his shoe.

Colin saw some yellow and pushed up front. Stza was dancing something like a jig on stage, rapping, "*incarcerate the youth of the next generation / and you get the high-fives at the police station.*" Colin screamed the lyrics for a few songs. Leftover Crack played "Born to Die," their usual closer—"*I just can't escape the lying / the moment we're born, we're dying*"—and right after that the venue people turned on the lights. The house music was death metal. Colin found Dana and they stood around for a while. They used the bathroom. They wandered to the outside area, where a girl was interviewing Stza.

"Alright," the girl was saying. She had bright orange hair and a large tape recorder, and was young, maybe in 8th grade. "So what's the point of what you're doing? What do you hope to gain?"

"Well, the point…" Stza said. "Actually we've pretty much done everything I had hoped to do. I wanted to be in a band, I wanted people to come to our shows. I didn't have a lot of friends growing up and I wanted to meet people… see, I'm really shy, and I just can't walk up to people and talk to them. I feel like a total jerk. But if kids come up to me and talk I can just talk back."

"Is this the one important thing about the band… that you are going to extremes just because you're making a point of free speech?"

"That's one of the things," Stza said. "But it's not the only reason I say some things. I mean a lot of the things I say. I joke about a lot of things. But only half joking."

"Is that why you have satanic imagery on your website? To be offensive?"

"Yeah, yeah. I mean, I'm an atheist. I like satanic art, I think it's pretty... I'm not a Satanist, but if you read the Satanic Bible, a lot of it is just common sense, really. It's not about hurting people, it's about freedom and autonomy."

One of the Polish women—the mom—was watching and had been moving closer and was now standing next to Stza. She asked about some beers that were sitting on a fence. "I wonder whose they are," she said. There were three beers.

"Don't know. You can have them," Stza said.

"No; you should have them. They're not mine."

"Thank you," Stza said.

"I wish someone would have them so they wouldn't just be sitting there."

"I'm sure someone will have them," Stza said.

"Okay. Goodbye." She turned to leave.

"Goodbye," Stza said. "Well, you know, I eat out of the garbage, so..."

The polish woman turned back around. "What?" she said.

"I eat out of the garbage, so it doesn't matter," Stza said. "A lot of kids do, so they'll drink the beers."

"I don't think they're garbage, I think they're sealed cans, just over there—look."

"I'll go check it out if it makes you happy," Stza said.

"Just chuck them over the fence into that garden."

"No! That's wrong," Stza said. "I don't believe in littering. This is such a pretty place."

"But someone might use them to throw at people's windows."

"They're empty aluminum cans, that's not going to break a window. I know these things."

"He's too smart for me," the woman said to Colin and Dana. She smiled at Colin. "Oh," Colin said, and looked away. Dana was holding his hand, he saw. "Will you put them in the bin for me then?" the Polish woman said. "They worry me."

"Alright," Stza said. "When we go back we have to go back that way—so we will." He looked around. The little girl with the orange hair was gone. She had vanished.

"Thanks," the woman said, "you're an angel."

"Thank you. An angel of death."

Outside the venue, the sky was a distinct brown. Kids pointed at it. "What the fuck is that?" someone said.

"It's a piece of doo-doo," someone screamed. There were clouds but those were brown too. A group of kids began to chant, "Don't dis the sky, don't dis the sky." No one wanted to go home. Everyone loitered in the street, kicked at snow, talked shit about Good Charlotte. Colin walked around a little and soon couldn't find Dana. He stood in one place, looking and shivering, feeling an unpleasant and comprehensive longing for tonight; it was a thousand years later and Colin was thinking back, remembering—regretting everything. But he would not be alive in one thousand years, he knew. He would be alone in a vast and unimaginable place. He felt a little confused. He saw Leftover Crack's bassist running away, sprinting down the block, slowing, turning a corner. Then a girl was asking Colin his name. "Colin," Colin said. "Hi," the girl said. She had round and vapid eyes and a very thin, silver hoop in her nose. "I'm Maura. Join me, Frank, Donnie in a Chinese dinner. We're going to Manhattan Chinatown. You're invited."

Dana walked up.

Maura introduced herself again. They talked briefly about a building across the street, then buildings in general. What if they got so tall that they broke off into outer space? "You two are together," Maura said after a while. "You aren't alone and feeling bad... feeling alone," she said to Colin. She gazed at them. "Things haven't changed. You're both invited."

The moon was fuzzy and it looked like it had snowed there too, or else it was a large piece of snow, falling slowly, carefully, in an orbit. It was the moon, and could do what it wanted.

"You two aren't very curious," Maura said. "Not a good sign. Hmm. Look. Frank and Donnie." She stepped aside, pointed behind her. Frank and Donnie were standing there, small and indistinct, down two or three blocks.

At the Chinese restaurant, Maura had an idea that everyone should spend all their money tonight; they'd found a homeless person on the train and he was here with them too—a short, bearded man who hadn't said anything. They put their money together, a little over a hundred dollars. Maura brought the cash to the large Chinese woman in charge of the place and asked her to order for them, and keep twenty percent for tip. A waiter appeared and engaged the Chinese woman in conversation without looking at her.

Dana's cell phone rang. It was her boyfriend and she said that she was going to go now, and stood up.

Colin wasn't thinking that he wouldn't ever see Dana again after tonight. He didn't think of that until after Dana had left. It was later, now, that Colin realized: when Dana was standing by the table, a few minutes ago, looking, she was waiting for him to stand up, so that they could say goodbye or something, exchange phone numbers maybe, but Colin had just sat there, without moving—had been thinking about Dana's film, about asking her where to meet tomorrow, if she was just being nice; then about how good and mysterious it was that Dana had held his hand earlier—and then she had come over, leaned down, hugged him, and left.

"I wonder if Stza masturbates to celebrities," Frank was saying. "What about to nine eleven? That's so dumb, when people say that. Getting off on nonsexual things, I hate that shit."

"He probably masturbates to the idea of masturbating to nine eleven," Donnie said. "He's one step ahead like that. That's how people are. There's like five steps, and you figure out what kind a person you are by what step you're on. Fuck you, Mrs. Johnson." He said to Colin, "Um, my math teacher. She was in my head just now. I was like, what are you doing…"

"What if someone wrote a song called 'Fuck Africa,' or something?" Frank said. He had a worried look on his face. "'Fuck Black People.' A song called 'Fuck Native Americans.'"

Maura was leaned over the table, her head low, and was gazing up, a bit blankly, at Colin. "Are you offended?" she said.

Colin shook his head no.

"You're crestfallen," Maura said.

"I'm not."

"Crestfallen?" Donnie said. "Nice. I like that. Romantic."

"What if Stza saw a slide," Frank said. "Like a playground slide. In a field somewhere. And he was alone and no one was watching—would he do it?"

"He'd probably hide in it—on top—and masturbate to the idea of hiding there and masturbating," Donnie said. "See how we're different? I'm on one step, you're on another, lower step. Me and Stza are pointing and laughing at you."

"No... because I'm being serious," Frank said. "I'm on an elevator or something, being serious."

"I'm operating your elevator," Donnie said. "Your elevator's a cardboard box. You live in a cardboard home and sit there being serious all day. At night, you make beastlike noises, you clutch your face in horror..." Donnie looked off to the side at something.

"He would—he'd do the slide," Frank said. "I wouldn't though. I'd be too apathetic. I'd be like, what difference does it make? Stza would be like, 'Hey, a slide.' Stza wouldn't get along with bin Laden." Frank was shaking his head. "Stza would be all sarcastic and bin Laden wouldn't get it. They'd just have all these awkward silences. Bin Laden would murder Stza in his sleep."

"Apathetic is pathetic with an 'A,'" Donnie said.

"Osama bin Laden," Maura said. "Ouch." Her head lay on its side, on her arms, on the table. Her eyes were closed. "I feel so alone when I close my eyes and talk. I hear my voice and everywhere else is this sad music, like, behind me." She began to hum, very quietly, "La-la-mm-mm-la, ah-ah-mm..."

"Did she say sad music or sad*istic* music?" Donnie said. He put his hand in the air. "Give me five," he said to Frank. "Give me a high-five for what I just said."

Frank looked at Donnie. "I wonder if bin Laden ever gets depressed," he said. "I'm serious. I think about this a lot. Depressed people... are so depressed and harmless. Bin Laden and everyone, Bush—they're always grinning on TV. What the fuck is that. No one ever thinks about this shit, really."

There was a metal rod inside of Colin. The rod went up from his stomach into the middle of his head. It was made of steel and sugar, and had been dissolving inside of Colin for ten or fifteen years, slow and sweet, above and behind his tongue; and he would taste it in that way, like an aftertaste, removed and seeping and outside of the mouth. Sometimes he'd glimpse it with the black, numb backs of his eyes. But what he really wanted was to wrench it out. Cut it up and chew it. Or melt it. Bathe in the hard, sweet lava of it.

Their food came. Three dishes, then three more, then a pot of something murky and deep. The large Chinese woman sat down with them. "I sense a new person," Maura said. "Hi." Her eyes were still closed. "It's the boss-lady," Donnie said. Maura sat up, opened her eyes, asked the Chinese woman about getting some more homeless people to come help eat. The Chinese woman laughed. She shouted something and the waiter left the restaurant on a bike.

The short homeless man was eating and so was Colin, but no one else.

"My phys-ed teacher-person called me 'homeslice' yesterday," Frank said. "What the hell is that? He kept doing it."

"He probably said he needed to go home and slice some pizza," Donnie said. "I'm going to go *home*, *slice* some pizza."

"No, he was like, 'Frank, homeslice, get over here and do twenty push-ups.'"

"You should've said, 'Your mom's a homeslice.' Then stayed where you were, doing zero push-ups."

"I feel depressed," Frank said.

"Do you know?" Maura said to Colin. "What is a homeslice? You're older than us. You're wiser."

"Crestfallen," Donnie said.

Colin looked up and shook his head. Blood moved slowly and disproportionately through his head, like a water and a syrup both. He concentrated on eating a piece of vegetable. It wouldn't fit in his mouth and he concentrated on that.

"You seem hungry," Maura said. "Are you under-nourished?"

"Are you a reporter?" Donnie said. "I've had this... bad vibe, that you're a reporter from USA Today. When I saw you, the headline came into my head, 'Teenage Terrorism Gangs at Punk Shows,' and it had a bar graph. I was like, that's not right, that's fucked up—the bar graph, I mean."

Frank began to eat. He had a damaged, pensive look on his face. He ate rice.

"I don't think you are," Maura said. "Your posture." She gazed at Colin. "Reporters wouldn't dare have your posture. Reporters have horse eyes. You have dog... bird eyes. You don't move your head to look at something, you move your eyes."

"I'm going to carpet bomb the Super Bowl with my al Qaeda friend, who lives on Second Avenue and…" Donnie said. He stared at Colin, who was looking down, at all the vegetables that he had moved onto his plate. There was a withered piece of carrot, a mushroom, a pile of baby corn, and an enormous green thing.

"Reporters aren't as hungry as you," Maura said.

Frank stood up. "I'm going to the bathroom to vomit," he said, and went there.

"I like you, Colin," Donnie said. He looked around. "I mean it. I usually hate all people. You should come to my birthday party next week. I don't have friends. Just these people here, and they don't even like me. Frank. Ha. I don't ever talk this much. I'm probably on anti-anxiety drugs right now. I'm always like, 'I hate you, what's the point of talking.' Or I'm walking around and I'm all like, 'I'm normal. I'm a normal person. Fuck all these weirdoes.' Really, I'm probably exactly like you. *Exactly*. You should see me at school. I stare at the wall. There's this wall. Anyway." His voice was wavering a bit. He took out a 3 x 5 note card and set it in front of Colin:

Donnie's birthday extravaganza
No clowns, no presents, no singing, fuck no, no
    cake, no nothing

Sure to be a depressing time for everyone involved
You shouldn't even come, please

The waiter came back with his bike and three other people—his twin, a tall and bearded man, and a tiny, wrinkled, peanut-colored woman. They pulled up another
table and sat down. The waiter went and got more soup
and bowls.

"These are gargantuan," the short homeless man
said. He held his bowl up to the light and everyone
looked. It was a normal-sized bowl.

The tall man smelled a little sour. He was sitting by
Colin, and now stood up. "Thank you, sir," he said to
Colin, and sat down.

Colin said something shocking yet compassionate,
but he wasn't sure what exactly—or if, even, as he did-
n't hear his own voice and also had been thinking about
something completely else.

"Thank you, Colin," the short man said.

"Thank you, Colin, sir," the tall man said.

The tiny, wrinkled woman was smiling very pleasantly. She had a little teacup in front of her. The waiter's twin had on a "NASA" hoodie and was talking to
Donnie. "We lived in Seattle then moved here. We've
written four film scripts each, eight in total. We have a

shared identity but we also have distinct individual identities. Well, what do you think?"

Frank came back. His face and hair were wet, his eyes were unfocused, and his seat had been taken. He stood there a while, then focused his eyes, put food on a plate, sat alone at an adjacent table, and ate.

"You're trying to say something," Maura said to the tiny, wrinkled woman, who was moving her lips in an unhurried, fishlike way. Some spit got onto her chin and she coughed a few times. Little coughs, like drops of water. Finally she very clearly and quickly said, "What are your movies about?" She did not have an accent. They were all looking at her.

"That depends. Wait... do you mean plotwise?" the waiter's twin said. "Wait," he said loudly.

They all continued looking at the tiny woman. She was very wrinkled. She began to cough again, then reached for a napkin and knocked over her teacup, which was filled with something not easily describable. It wasn't tea. There was food in it, and a small mound of sugar or something. "Oh shit," she said, softly and without agitation, and then carefully stood and walked slowly out of the restaurant.

"I think what she meant?" the waiter said, looking at his twin. "Was overall, as in what are our preoccupations?"

"Life," the twin said quickly. He stared at his brother, the waiter. "What, you don't think so? I hesitated earlier. I shouldn't have. We're different."

Maura stood. "Let's go help her," she said, and pulled Colin up. As she and Colin left, the waiter was saying, "She's not as old as you think. She uses the internet, you know? Friendster?"

It was snowing outside. Colin felt cold, but in a stony, immune way. He was a marble statue, unearthed after a hundred million years—fascinating. The woman stood on the corner, small and shoulderless as a penguin. The wind lifted her hair above her head, like a small, white flame.

"We'll each hold one of her arms," Maura said. They went and did that.

Maura leveled her face with the woman's and asked where they were going, then positioned her ear directly in front of the woman's mouth. Maura's nose ring was very bright. Colin stared at it and could hear it shining. It was a noise like a happy person waking from a nap—continually waking from a nice nap.

The woman pointed across the street. There was a McDonald's, glowing yellow and red in complex, ongoing, and freakish acknowledgement of itself. As they crossed the street, Colin couldn't see that well; snow moved elaborately toward his face, in curlicues and from below. But he felt that he could hear better. He could hear their six shoes sloshing against the snow. It was a crumbling noise, he realized, only faster.

Inside McDonald's it was very warm. They sat in a booth by the entrance. The woman said she wanted an Oreo McFlurry, but had no money.

"You don't need money," Maura said. "Don't move." She stood and went to the back, to the ordering counter.

The woman began to shiver. Colin took off his jacket and put it on her back. She touched her ears. "It's cold here," she said. "These places." She touched her forehead and eyebrows.

Colin pulled the jacket up, covering her head completely. It looked like it put an uncomfortable weight on her neck. Colin slid in close, right next to her, and held the jacket up a little.

"That's pretty good," the woman said. "I don't like the city. No, never. Don't ask me that." She began to talk faster and louder. "I'm moving to the Florida Keys. I'm not driving. I'm taking a plane. I'm living in a hut on the beach." She paused, then coughed.

"Oh," Colin said.

"Everyone's doing something and that's what a city is," the woman said. "I'm old. I don't want to communicate at the speed of light on Mars. My daughter died in the towers. She didn't need to be there, typing, doing things at the speed of light. Not my daughter but other daughters. I mean—people. Something. I can't get at the things in my head. They're tiny. They move too slow." She was coughing or sobbing now—or both; there was a sound like two or three hamsters squeaking. Colin leaned over to look at her face, but it was just a shadow under the jacket, an abyss. "Where were you when the towers happened?" she said.

"Sleeping."

"Singing? What?"

"Sleeping."

"Oh, that's good. So don't wake up. Build a home by a beach. Leave the city and get a bed. Those are important. Beds. Don't wake up through any of this, ever. Don't dream about cities or progress. Don't wake up or dream. That's what I'm saying. Is that wrong? What should I say then? It's too late to say anything."

"It's... what time is it?" Colin said inaudibly.

Maura came back holding a McFlurry and with a McDonald's manager following her. She set the McFlurry down and sat opposite the woman and Colin. The McFlurry had some ice cream smeared on its outside and no cap on top.

The manager stood by the booth. "None of you have money?" he said. He was extremely tall and was staring down at Colin. "I believe that. I'm not self-right-eous. Listen," he said. He stared at Colin without blink-ing. "Okay. Listen. 'From anyone who takes away your coat, do not withhold even your shirt. Give to everyone who begs from you, and if anyone takes away your goods, do not ask for them again.' Listen; just keep lis-tening. 'Students of Buddha should not take pleasure in being honored, but should practice detachment...'" He continued on like that.

Colin's eyes were very dry. He was staring back at the manager, wide-eyed, and when he finally blinked, both his contact lenses crinkled and fell out, onto his cheeks. He brushed them quickly off his face.

The manager stopped talking and affected a sudden, neutral expression. He stared at Colin's contact lenses, which were on the table.

"Do you need something for those?" the manager said slowly. "Yeah. I think you need alcohol solution to clean them, now that they're dirty."

"It's good to not wear them sometimes, for a change," Maura said. "Once a year... week."

They were all looking at the contact lenses, which were squirming a little, slowly unfolding.

The old woman was weeping and coughing very quietly.

Colin brushed at the contact lenses until they fell off the table. He was blushing hard and was sweating a little in some places. He rested his hands in his lap, and felt them there—light as gloves, gentle and dead as birds.

The manager took from his pocket a colorful wad of Monopoly money. He stuffed that quickly back in his pocket, then took a five-dollar bill from another pocket. "Here," he said. He set it on the table, looked at it, flattened it out. "That's five… real dollars." He smiled and looked very happy. He smiled less after a while, then renewed his smile, then left.

"People can be so nice," Maura said. She was looking at the woman. "Maybe you shouldn't eat that freezing-cold… you're shivering. You're hyperventilating."

The woman moved the McFlurry into the dark area below the jacket and the weeping noise stopped.

Maura climbed over the table and held the woman. She set the side of her head lightly against the woman's back and closed her eyes. "I've wanted to ask about your friend Dana," she said after a while. It was snowing very hard outside; snow was flying against the glass then vanishing, quiet and rescued as the tiny ghosts of baby doves. Everything else outside was a lucid and excited black. "What do I want to know?" Maura said. "I don't know. Something." She began to hum loudly.

Colin had been thinking about the week after September 11th, had been thinking about that for a long time—but wasn't anymore. He wasn't thinking anything anymore. He was the effect of some inception. There was the first thing, and then so on, all the rest being effect, and there was nothing Colin could do about that. If he was going to feel this way, then he was going to feel this way. Feelings were a part of the effect too. The effect was everything, and forever. It couldn't be changed or gotten out of.

But Colin wasn't thinking or feeling any of this, really.

It was all just there, in him—what he'd think or feel if he were to. It was a leaf, waiting for him. His heart was a leaf. A white leaf, inside a gigantic noise.

September 11th, that Tuesday, Colin had called Dana's room and left a message. He called again the next day and left another. It was the second week of college and Colin didn't know anyone. He spent that week lying awake in his room, listening to music, not eating barely anything. Mostly just thinking about Dana. Waiting for her call.

By Friday, Colin had convinced himself that Dana hadn't called because she had left the city; a lot of people had—his roommate had. Though, really, he wasn't sure, as he'd been thinking about when they last hung out. It had been different than the times before. They hadn't had fun really—not nearly as much as at first—and hadn't made plans. But then maybe she had just left the city.

It wasn't until a few months later—after Dana met her boyfriend—that Colin found out she had been across Washington Square Park all that week; she hadn't left, hadn't called.

But that was later.

On Friday, Colin could still feel a little less lonely thinking about Dana.

That night they were showing movies for free at Union Square, and Colin went. There were many homeless people, all of them alone. No one wanted to sit by a homeless person—with their puffy, Godless coats; their animal largeness—but then every seat filled, and some people had to. Colin was a little dazed, watching this, and had stopped, for a time, feeling sorry for himself, but for everyone else—everything. The movie was very independent and very sad. Outside, the streets were closed to cars. People walked on them. Missing-person flyers were taped over ads and poles. It was very quiet without any cars. Colin felt vast and detailless and disembodied; it was the same tired and endless feeling everywhere, he felt, inside of him and out—in the stung and ashen air, the buildings tall and pale as apparitions, the strange and lowered sky. Colin didn't want to go back to his room. He walked around for a very long time, looking down at the sidewalks and streets, and thought of the things he and Dana might say to each other if she were with him. And every once in a while he would catch himself smiling and laughing a little, and it was those moments right after—as, having lapsed into fantasy, there was a correction, a moment of nothing and then a loose and sudden rush, back into the real world in a trick of escape, as if to some new place of possibilities—that he felt at once, and with clarity, most exhilarated, appreciative, disappointed, and accepting.

Nine, Ten

People got a bit careless that year. Band-aids were for-
gone, small wounds allowed to go a little out of control—to infect a bit. Jobs were quit. People woke early-
evening or mid-afternoon, fisted ice cream bars, wandered from their homes—only a little bit depressed—
and walked diagonally through parking lots. They felt
no longer in the midst of things, but in the misty *after-
math* of things, the quaint and narcotic haze of what
comes after. A haze in which nothing, they knew, could
ever fully, truly, happen. Anything there was could only
yearn for itself, at a distance, behind barricades, could

only long for the real self of itself. The core of things—of love and life, of any simple feeling or thought—could no longer be experienced center-on, could no longer be thought of or felt directly, but only in trying, in tics and glimpses, in ways holographic and fleeing.

And so people stayed inside mostly. Some disappeared. Others called up their local papers, phoned in their own deaths and, next day, read their own obituaries with a strange, hollow sort of longing, a real but feeble passion for their alternate, dead selves. They sat nights in bathtubs, whistling, blow-drying their hair—*taking that risk*. They began exploring their own houses. Moving things around and touching stuff, as they had begun to sense that there was something with them, unseen and poignant, something slightly alive and, they suspected, relevant, inside the walls or behind the furniture, a thing cloaked and shadowy that approached, in angles, and then vanished—*their own lives*, they came to realize. It was their own lives, living with them, playing games, tag and hide-and-seek, and—having hid somewhere good, somewhere *unfindable*, years ago probably—stubborn, wanting to be found, needing that resolution, but just rotting there, then, in whatever godforsaken hiding spot, like some mean, oversweet piece of fruit, spurned, finally, to a crisp—an apple chip.

In the oceans, sea life grew bold. Sharks leapt into boats, snarling, leapt out. Tuna fish matured to the size of small whales, and packs of seals moved inland, taking the back roads. All along the coasts were suicides, rare and wintry specimens—narwhal, whale sharks, oarfish—beaching themselves, rolling up far (*too far*, people said), sliding onto the grassier sands, scooting up against the beachfront hotels, the Slurpy huts.

At Cocoa Beach, there was the oversized squid. It was early summer and Florida, and the squid washed smoothly ashore—forty-feet long and pink-flecked—in one extra-foamy wave.

"Architeuthis dux," people said. "The giant squid." They were knowledgeable. They had their patterned towels, their wine coolers, and they moved down the beach in a migratory trudge. "First the toe thing, the dog thing," said one woman, looking around, "last week the toaster, after that the cow, then the ticks, the little apocalypse, the parking lot with the political skater punks, now this squid thing, this squid... thing."

Her face had gotten red and she lightly slapped it a few times, after which she looked a little better—mollified.

Jed, his dad, and his friend LJ were there. LJ was a girl and she and Jed were nine.

"That's interesting," Jed's dad said. But he wouldn't look at it—*the squid*. The three of them had a beach ball, were kicking it, and Jed's dad just kept kicking. He didn't know if he was ready for something like that, a thing of such size and agony. He might get obsessed—he was prone to—and also he had lately been practicing, earnestly, a kind of halfhearted Buddhism, with timeouts and the occasional off-day. He was to destroy almost all desires. He wasn't ready yet to destroy *all* desires. It scared him, actually, the idea of having no desires—as that in itself was a desire. Or was it? He didn't know, that was the thing. He was unemployed.

"Why don't we look at it from closer?" Jed said quietly. He would go himself, but it could be a trick—Venus flytrap or something. He didn't want to be mauled, not like some deer.

They kept kicking the beach ball.

Between kicks they had to stand there and wait, as the ball, once in the air, seemed to slow down, to take its time up there, enjoying the view.

The sky was blue until you looked into it, then you saw it was more of a lightly polluted gray.

"It's just a giant squid," LJ said after a while, having zoned out for some time. She now could see it looming, burrito-y and soulless, in her periphery. "It's just a giant squid," she said again. She kicked the ball, and then felt stupid. *It's just a giant squid*. What did she mean? She was just a little girl, she knew. "Wait," she whispered. She blushed. A wind came at her face and she had to blink a few times. A wave came, took back the squid, and deposited in its place a clump of dead jellyfish—the squashed, opaque bags of them like mangled eyes, flayed and beaten, swollen to the size of heads.

Another wave came and put the squid back on the beach.

That night Jed slept over at one of LJ's houses—she had two. They both dreamt of giant squid.

In Jed's dream he was a tiny shrimp, a krill. He floated in blackness and was confused. A giant squid went by slowly. Jed saw the eye, which was jazzy and glowing, like a TV and a moon both. He whispered in his krill's head, *hi*. He then felt such a crushing kind of weakness that he began to tremble, as if he might soon cease to exist.

In LJ's dream she kept saying, "It's just a giant squid." Each time she said it, she felt a little stupider. Finally, she started to cry. Jed kept kicking the beach ball, but only at his dad, except once at the giant squid; the ball bounced smoothly off, then back to Jed, who kicked it smoothly to his dad. At one point, also, the squid mimicked LJ—unkindly, she thought. *It's just a giant squid*, it said. Then it made a noise. LJ was taken aback because the noise was very unsquidlike.

In the morning, the squid was on the local news.

"Lewly," LJ's mom said to LJ. "You went here yesterday?" She looked at Jed. She was in love with Jed's dad. They were both divorced from unmemorable people, and both had high metabolism. They had dated each other awhile—after she won the lottery a few years back, moved from Canada to Florida, and bought two houses—but it hadn't worked out. "Jed," she said. She pointed at the TV, which had an aura of rinky-dink, somehow-charming totalitarianism. "You were here yesterday. Don't lie to me."

Jed nodded.

"Veteran seafarers have measured them at 200 feet," the TV was saying. It showed a veteran seafarer, and the newsman grinned. The screen changed. It showed a prostrate man, a school bus, two giant squid—one 60 feet, one 200 feet. At the bottom, it had a row of exclamation marks.

"I like exclamation marks," LJ said. She wasn't so sure, though. She only liked them sometimes. "I don't like exclamation marks," she said. She shook her head. "No," she said. Things could bother LJ in this way. Both she and her mom were readers. Her mom claimed to read not for pleasure, but to confirm her worldview. LJ herself had a questionable way of reading. She would flip through, read a sentence here, a sentence there. If she didn't like a sentence, she'd pick another. Finally, she'd feel *done*, and then would look, with confidence, at the cover, to make up her own story. She had read much of Vonnegut, and a third of Kafka.

"Nova Scotia," Jed said slowly. The night before, he and LJ had looked up giant squid on the internet. "Ink sac," he mumbled.

"Those squid," LJ's mom said. "200 feet! Those damn squid!" She was standing. She stood when watching TV, did stretching exercises, sometimes touched the TV screen—usually with a middle finger. "What do they think they're doing? Jed, what are they doing?"

Things could do what they wanted, Jed thought. "They're just growing," he said very quietly.

"You could feed a small country with one of those squid," LJ's mom said. "For a week. I bet you could do that. Maybe not. A small town then. A small, Welsh village." She looked at LJ and smiled, then back at the TV. "You've got to be specific," she said. "A small, seventeenth-century, Welsh village."

LJ was staring off to the side, eyes unfocused. She was thinking about Nova Scotia. She liked Nova Scotia. Sometimes, in bed, under the covers and comfy, she'd think that she felt very Nova Scotic. She had dreamed, once, of dining Italian with Nova Scotia. Nova Scotia had a small mouth, was a wind-blown arctic wolf, tall and groomed and soft-spoken, and had ordered something with eggplant. LJ had read a book on Nova Scotia.

The three of them stood there, in front of the TV, which had moved on—it had a lot to get to—was now warning of deadly substances that sometimes dripped from rain gutters. A man had been killed, and some animals, allegedly. It showed a photo of a man, a dog, and a hamster that looked, for a hamster, alarmingly distraught.

"My god!" LJ's mom said. "That hamster!" She loved TV. She really did. TV excited her, rejuvenated her, entered her like something kindhearted and many-handed that held her up, then hardened into a kind of scaffolding. The TV had segued into hamsters and was showing a slideshow of them, each one badly deranged in the face. It kept showing more and more hamsters, and LJ's mom began to feel sad. As a child, she had one afternoon been diagnosed—*condemned,* she sometimes thought—with Asperger Syndrome, social anxiety disorder, bipolar disease, and a few other things. It was a turning point, that day, she knew. Her life had been going in one direction, cruising, windows down, but then had turned, taken a left through a redlight, gunned it; had later run out of gas in a kind of desert outside of town. These days she was staying inside mostly. She had won the lottery, moved from Canada to Florida. She was writing a book, actually.

"What if you could Google your own house?" Jed murmured. "If you lost your keys or TV remote you could just Google it."

LJ's mom looked at Jed. She walked to him. "What did you just say? Can you repeat that?" She leaned down and carefully moved her ear to Jed's mouth.

Jed concentrated on loudness and clarity, and then repeated what he had said.

LJ's mom stood and smiled. "Oh, Jed," she said. "That's wonderful."

"Oh," Jed said. It annoyed him that people couldn't ever understand what he was saying. He looked around for LJ, who had wandered into the kitchen.

LJ's mom patted Jed's head and looked outside, through her sliding glass door. The swimming pool was covered—you couldn't see the water—with mulch, moss, and leaves; it looked very much like a swamp, actually, had large, cage-y branches floating in it, as a tree had fallen through the screen some time ago and LJ's mom had liked that, the idea of it, so had left it there. There was a squirrel, now, by the pool, standing motionless in that clicked-in way of the lower animals. The sun shone brightly on its handsome face. LJ's mom stared out there, feeling a bit blighted, here inside, some-how cheated. She was thinking that if she married Jed's dad and LJ became Jed's girlfriend, how wonderful that would be. They'd all live together in a little house some-where, with a shiny roof, atop some green hill. It would be in New Zealand, she thought, feeling precarious, or else Wisconsin.

Jed's dad began to learn, that year, to enjoy waiting; there was something true and mastered about it, he knew—the casual excellence of waiting—that could induce you, lead you focusedly deathward, like a drug addiction, but without the frenzy or desperation. He felt, at times, that he could wait for anything—a month, a year, a thousand years—for love or friendship or happi-ness. He could exist like a theory in the place before the real place, could float there in the pigeon flight of pre-ambition, in a kind of gliding, thinking only small things and feeling only small emotions, pre-pathos, so that you could fit your entire life easily in your head, and carry it around, like a pleasant memory from some wholesome childhood, yours or someone else's, it didn't matter.

"LJ said Jed was being held back a year," LJ's mom said to Jed's dad on the phone. Jed's dad had liked her at first. They had gone to the movies, bowling, arcades with the kids. But over time he had seen something selfish in her, something a bit insane. She could be jealous and unreasonable. One night she had thrown a potted plant. And though he now sometimes suspected that she was a good, caring, sane person, that it was *he* who just hadn't tried hard enough, who wasn't accommodating and tolerant enough, he had stopped calling her, then, after the potted plant. But she had kept calling him.

"You shouldn't let that happen," LJ's mom said. "You can't, responsibility-wise."

"It's okay," Jed's dad said. In the elementary schools, they had begun to hold back entire ostensible playgroups of children, bunches of them, together, like something tethered and collective-brained. Jed and everyone who seemed to sit nearby this one big-headed kid, seven of them, all the foreboding, quiet kids—you could never tell if they were slow or gifted—were to repeat the fourth grade.

"It's not okay," LJ's mom said. "I know Jed. Jed's smart. You know this. They, though—they don't know this. It's just a misunderstanding, to be corrected." She began to worry that Jed and LJ would drift apart if LJ advanced to the fifth grade without Jed. "What are you going to do?"

"People are different," Jed's dad said. "I think..." He didn't think anything, but began to feel a little as if everything was futile.

"Have them test him. This isn't right. I mean—repeating the fourth grade, it can do things. I knew this girl, she was held back. After that she kept getting held back. They got carried away. They pulled her all the way back to Kindergarten, then expelled her from the public school system. Her parents had to pay a series of fines to get her into pre-school." She laughed a little. Beakers were going through her mind; a hand, calmly placing beakers onto a resplendent oak table. She didn't know why. Probably something from TV. She had, as usual, taken a caffeine pill half-an-hour before calling Jed's dad. "It's strange," she said, "how they don't care anymore. People, I mean. Me too. All of us. We've no illusions anymore. People need illusions. Do you know what I'm talking about? What do you think?"

"It's not bad," Jed's dad said. He hesitated these days to say anything about the world, to have any opinions or beliefs. Anything spoken was a lie, he knew—anything in the mind was a lie. What was *out there* was what was true. Once your mind got involved, everything turned to lies. You had just to exist, to be passive and apathetic as a dead thing in the sea, as there was a private, conspiratorial truth to just not doing anything, a kind of coming-to-terms, a loneliness turned contentment, a sort of friendliness towards oneself. Or was there? When was something completely made up and when was something only a little made up? Jed's dad knew never to trust himself. Think too hard, he knew, and you found that there was no point in saying, thinking, or doing anything.

"It is, though," LJ's mom said. "It's bad. You know it. No one's planning for the long-term anymore. The generation before us, they said things. They said…" She couldn't think of anything. "They said a lot of things. Now the Earth is—let's face it—doomed. I saw on TV, they're rethinking one of the smaller continents as a garbage dump, *reinterpreting* it, they said. I mean, wow. And what are they doing with the moon? Shouldn't we be living on the moon in those space domes by now? Scouting the outer planets? I mean, what year is this? What is the government *doing* these days? NASA, whatever?" She thought briefly about the Ort Cloud—it was coming, but what *was* it? "Why don't you come over?" she said. "I'll make food. I have new recipes. I'll cook." She wanted to talk, just wanted to keep on talking, for hours, *forever,* wanted to argue and discuss things, any kind of thing, as she couldn't talk to anyone like this, only to kids, and to Jed's dad—with other people she just felt alone in the world and nauseated—but he wasn't saying anything.

"Next week then," LJ's mom said. "Saturday. Saturday, okay? Jed and everyone."

"Okay," Jed's dad said. "We'll see."

They were in their late twenties, had both married young, to early girl and boyfriends, were both aware of the basic eschatology of things, though in different ways. Jed's dad could sense the end of life as a place you got to, someplace far away and separate, like Hawaii; could sometimes see it, that it was a nice place, with trees, a king-size bed. LJ's mom couldn't sense that place. Hers was the view—the experience—that every moment was a little death, that you were never really alive, because you were always dying. And in this way she sensed, instead, everything swirling around her, felt the slow-fast blur of each moment, the raking of it, the future grinding through her, to the past, and crashing, at times, like a truck, through her skull. Sometimes, walking around the house or doing whatever, she would suddenly feel smashed in the head, with sadness or disbelief or some other disorienting method. Days would go by, then, weeks or months, before she recovered.

The next Saturday Jed's dad decided to stay home. He sent Jed over to LJ's. LJ's mom was quiet. Her face glowed lightly with make-up. They had bok choy with garlic sauce, broiled zucchini, and smoothies. LJ's mom had set up a table in the driveway, and that's where they

ate. LJ had one piece of zucchini and she put some garlic sauce on it. She was full after that. She couldn't finish her peach smoothie and was a little embarrassed.
"It's okay," LJ's mom said, and petted LJ's head. After
eating, they watched *Titanic*, the recent remake of it,
animated and not so epic, from the point-of-view of an
indignant family of bottom-dwelling fish, made further
indignant by the leveling of their known world by the
Titanic. Jed went home and LJ went to sleep. LJ's mom
cleaned up. She watched *Titanic* again, wept briefly at
the end—where the father fish is mutilated by a plastic
six-pack ring—and then went across the street, to her
other house.

She hadn't furnished it yet. The electricity wasn't
working. It was dark and warm and she went soberly
through each of the rooms, then upstairs. She took off her
sandals. The carpet was nice and thick and soft. "House
two," she said to her feet. It amused her only a little to
own two houses. Not nearly enough, she felt. It should
amuse her more. She went to a window, looked across
the street at her other house. She watched her own front
door. She wanted to see herself come out from there,
come skipping across the street; wanted to see what she
looked like from above; and wanted, then, to meet herself on the stairs—surprise herself—and give herself a

hug. "Susan," she shouted. "Susan Anne Michaels! What are you doing…" She turned and looked at the room she was in. She did a cartwheel across it, into a sit, and sat there, Indian-style. Through the window she could see the space-dried clay of the moon, blanched as deep white space, blemished as a coin. She stood and went downstairs. She heard some noises, became frightened, and then ran home, to her other house.

She lay on her gigantic bed, stomach-down and splay-limbed. She felt plain. She thought of getting drunk or something. Maybe she should dye her hair. She began to adjust the hardness of her mattress; she had bought one of those mattresses. There was a fact out there, she felt, that she didn't know. This was a fact that you had to know in order to live. There was a knowing to being alive, and she just didn't know. She closed her eyes, listened to the little mattress motor, working hard, and began to think on her life, tracing it forward and back in a squiggled, redundant way. She thought, without much conviction, that if she concentrated hard enough, if she started, carefully, in her childhood and moved forward, gaining momentum, then when she reached the present moment she might be able to turn it, her life, like a pipe cleaner, might be able to twist it, attitudinally, in some new and pleasant direction.

"Well do it then," she said loudly, in her head.

She would have to start with her first memory. It was a photo of herself, a tiny girl. Her next memory was of being embarrassed—her face red, the world terrible. She moved on. She needed momentum. She couldn't focus on anything, so she skipped to tonight, to watching *Titanic*. She went through the movie, went through going to her house across the street, and then thought of what she was doing one minute ago—she was going through *Titanic*. She began to go through that again. She got confused. She thought of the moment immediately before the present, the confusion, thought of the present, and then thought forcefully ahead. Things got blank. She felt herself lying on the bed.

In the morning Jed went back to LJ's.

LJ's mom set two bowls of cereal and soy milk on the counter. She went into the living room, picked up a book, and stood reading in front of the TV.

In the kitchen, Jed and LJ went for pop tarts. LJ licked hers, the frosted front of it. Jed bit his. They watched each other while eating. LJ's tongue was small and pink, like a puppy's.

"Listen to this," LJ's mom said from the living room. She read aloud from her book. "'Rather than using two dolls to play "dollies have tea," an autistic child might take the arm off one doll and simply pass it back and forth between her own hands.'"

Jed looked at LJ. She was very beautiful. In bed sometimes Jed would be thinking, *Lewly J*, and he wouldn't be able to sleep. He would sit and fluff his pillow and smooth his blanket. Sometimes he wanted badly to hold her. He'd move close to her and his insides would start going faster, everything spilling and cold against his bones and organs. He wondered sometimes if he had special powers, like the X-men. Not everyone was the same, Jed knew.

LJ heard in her head the unsquidlike noise from her dream. It was abrupt and bovine, and it startled her. She dropped her pop tart. She picked it up. The pop tart was beginning to wetly bend. She wasn't hungry, she knew. She was never hungry for breakfast or for lunch. It always took until dinner for her to get hungry. She blushed. She put the pop tart in the sink and used a spatula to shove it down the drain.

Jed wandered away, into some other room—the piano room—wanting LJ to follow. Chopin, Jed thought. Chopin was about five feet tall. His head was very big. Jed knew Chopin from his dad. His dad for some time had been obsessed with both Chopin and Glenn Gould. Jed once asked who would win in a fight,

Chopin or Glenn Gould. His dad had said it would take three Chopin's to beat up Glenn Gould. Jed liked Chopin.

LJ followed slowly into the piano room. She was thinking about when she had gotten a thin Chinese noodle accidentally inside of her head, up through her sinuses, out through a space below her eye. Her mom had pulled it out and then everything was okay.

"Let's go to the church," Jed said.

"Okay," LJ said. She was grinning. She ran and pushed Jed and Jed fell on the carpet. Jed stood and went to push LJ, but didn't know where on her body to. She was very small. Her head was wispy. It seemed almost invisible.

LJ screamed, a bit quietly, "We're going out!"

She had trouble opening the front door. Jed helped.

Outside, it was dewy and warm. LJ felt momentarily underwater, then as if in a sweltering place, a jungle or Africa. She looked around, unsure of things. "What if I climbed this tree?" she said. There was a tree, and they looked at it.

"It looks hard to," Jed said after a while.

"I'm not sure if I should," LJ said. She felt strange. For a moment it seemed to her that the day was already over—she was in bed, asleep, and then it was the next day and now here she was again. "Oh," she said.

They began walking. There was an empty lot where you could climb the neighborhood wall, on the other side of which was a fort built by some older kids and then a field, with a church and a McDonald's on it. They saw Jason, who had a green apple and was eating it. Jason was one grade more than them. "Where are you going?" Jason asked LJ. He looked at Jed.

"The church," Jed said.

Jason turned around and walked with them, adjacent LJ. He was tall. "Do you like me?" he said loudly to LJ. Someone had once told LJ that if asked, if given the choice, you were always to say yes. Probably her mom had said that. Her mom had said that if things ever got too bad it was okay to do drugs, as long as you kept reading Chuang Tzu the entire time. After she said that she had looked very worried.

"Yes," LJ said. She had the word *insalubrious* going through her head. She didn't know what it meant. Things were always going through her head like this. Things going through her head, herself going through the world; sometimes she got confused. She felt sleepy.

Jed saw in his periphery that Jason was holding LJ's hand. He thought that he should have held LJ's hand first, when they left the house; he was always too slow. But he wasn't the kind of person to make others uncomfortable, he knew. He felt good about that. But it was a tiny feeling, and not altogether a good one either.

At the empty lot, Jason ran at the wall and climbed it and stood on top. "Nostradamus predicted the world ended already," he said. "And it did. I can feel it in my brain. It feels like sand." He stood on one foot. He almost fell and his face reddened. He helped LJ and they went over.

Jed moved an empty bucket and used that and got over. He watched LJ and Jason go into the field. He felt like he was vanishing, that he had vanished. But then he was back again. He hadn't vanished. He went into the fort area. On a board of wood in green marker it said, "You're a butthead."

"I'm a butthead," Jed whispered. His heart beat a little faster. At the end of fourth grade, some kids had begun to say "Shit" and "Bitch." Jed didn't like it. They just said those things to be cool. Jed liked "Moron," and "Idiot." There was one kid who said "Moron" all the time and Jed secretly admired him. Jed liked anyone who was weak or quiet. You had to be weak, or else you were mean. You couldn't be mean, Jed knew. You could only be nice, and if you felt hurt you could only be even more nice.

It was getting cloudy. Jed picked up a branch and whacked some leaves off a tree. In first grade, he was sitting in the school auditorium and someone had called his name and he had gone to the front and received an award for a painting he had done. In the painting the sun was just a dot, you couldn't even see it. He was so weird then, he thought. He didn't know that person, his old self. It was as if for a long time, he didn't even have thoughts—wasn't aware of anything.

He walked outside the fort and saw that LJ and Jason were far away in the field. He wanted to go home. He wanted to teleport home, without having to do any work. You weren't supposed to be in a field during a storm, he knew. LJ and Jason looked to Jed like husband and wife. Jed always felt younger than his peers, like a baby almost. There was always the feeling that he had to try really hard at everything—smile bigger, talk louder and clearer, argue and fight things behind his eyes more. He thought that tonight he would read *PC Gamer* magazine and drink fruit punch with ice cubes in it while taking a bath. He liked computer games. He felt better. He ran into the field. As he neared LJ and Jason, he remembered hazily his mother—she had left when Jed was three—and felt almost like he was LJ and Jason's son. He ran to them.

"It's Jed," Jason said. "Jed head."

"Jason," Jed said inaudibly. He looked at Jason and LJ holding hands and felt very nervous. He looked away. The grass was up to their knees and Jed was afraid of snakes. They seemed to be walking toward McDonald's and not the church.

LJ began to wrap her hair around her neck. She had very thin smoke-brown hair. She hadn't been mentally focused for a while now. She had been thinking about… she couldn't remember what.

"Don't," Jason said. "You'll choke to death." He went to unwrap LJ's hair from her neck.

They stopped walking. LJ let Jason unwrap her hair some. What was happening, she thought. She twisted away and fell. She sat and looked at the top of the grass covering the rest of the field, swaying light green and flaxen, a failed and reoriented sea. "You'll choke to death on a stiff Chinese dumpling," she said. She grinned at Jed, who was looking down and doing a kind of sideways walk—shifting, it seemed. LJ didn't understand it.

Jason put a hand out as if to help LJ up. "A stiff Chinese dumpling," he said. "You don't know what that means." He was pointing now. With his other hand he took out an apple and began to nibble at it. "You can't act this way. You won't," he said. "When you know the world ended already you'll be different."

"That's the most meaningless thing I've ever heard," LJ said. She sat Indian-style. She widened her eyes and looked up at Jason and shouted, "What are you looking at?" Her voice was normally small; louder, now, it sounded a little like singing. Jason's face turned red, and LJ felt bad, and blushed. She had thought she was just playing. She didn't know.

"A dumpling," Jason said. "That's bad. That's racist." He threw his apple into the air and it went into the sky. He ran towards McDonald's.

A cloud moved and blocked the sun.

"Aren't you afraid of snakes?" Jed said. He spun in place, 360 degrees. One time LJ whispered in his ear that she liked him and he didn't believe her.

Snakes, LJ thought. She didn't know what that was. She remembered the squid. She would probably have to apologize soon. *It's just a giant squid*. She wasn't thinking when she said that. They should have gone and looked at it, and sat on it. "Gigantic squid are good," she said, and lay back into the grass. Jed felt afraid and went and looked down at her.

LJ's eyes were slowly moving. She was looking at the air, which seemed grayish, a little outer-space-y—but bright, too, because of the little dusts of light that were traveling through it. Her mom had told her that there wasn't ever any reason to worry about anything or be sad. Her mom had said that everything you ever did was a result of the thing that happened right before, because of cause and effect, and that that went on forever, going back, so that there wasn't ever a first thing, and there wouldn't ever be a last thing, and in between there was just the middle, and there you were, always, right in the middle, and you couldn't stop or change anything—so you didn't have to.

"It's dangerous. You're surrounded," Jed said, very slowly, concentrating as he spoke. "There are bugs on the ground. It's dirty."

LJ began to roll in the grass. She giggled, quietly and forcelessly—the sound of it like something you heard in your head after the first sound from outside.

"Don't!" Jed said. He thought of anthills and Indian arrowheads. "Stop that!" He felt a little dizzy, being so loud. LJ stood and quickly hugged Jed, then stepped back. "You're funny," she said. "You're weird." She was smiling.

Jed looked at her. His heart felt tiny and slippery—and sealed, like a marble, like it wouldn't ever get any bigger, wouldn't ever be able to pump enough blood. LJ pushed Jed's shoulder and ran away. After about twenty feet, she stopped and turned around. She took out a bonnet from her pocket and put it on her head. It was a black bonnet. She grinned and widened her eyes. She looked surprised. How pretty she was, it made Jed feel—not good or bad, but just feel, like it was something in him that was opening up, something new and secret, that only he would ever know, and he could fill it with sadness or longing or whatever, but here it was, opening centerless and vacuum-y as something attempting itself, and it would be over soon, and nothing, then, really, would've happened.

LJ ran back towards the wall, and it began to rain.

They both had colds for awhile. LJ's mom phoned Jed's dad, talked about colds and the flu. Jed's dad wasn't saying anything and after a while LJ's mom said, "What am I even doing right now?" She waited a second then hung up, and didn't call again until late in July, on a hot Sunday night; Jed answered.

"I'm drunk," she said, "I'm doing a hundred ten on the highway."

"LJ?" Jed said. He knew it wasn't LJ.

"Jed. Oh Jed," LJ's mom said. "What's going to happen to you?"

Jed's dad picked up on another line. Jed went into his room and sat on the carpet. He was frightened. What *was* going to happen to him? He took out some computer game magazines and looked at them, but couldn't concentrate.

"Think about LJ," Jed's dad said to LJ's mom. "Your daughter LJ. Your family."

"It doesn't matter," LJ's mom said. "That's nothing, that's nothingness. I don't care. What does a nihilist do? That's what I am, a nihilist. I don't know things. There isn't one thing out there that I *know*. Oh, now what. Now what! My car is shaking, my god, what kind of a car shakes. I'm going ninety, I'm slowing down." She was only a little drunk. Actually, she had had just one beer. But she hadn't slept. She hadn't been sleeping at all.

"I'll talk to you," Jed's dad said. He just didn't want to be in a relationship. He wanted to live ethereally, intrinsically, not doing anything—like a plant. He just didn't find people appealing anymore, not LJ's mom at least. He liked the monosyllabic, deadpan type, he knew, the type that withdrew when angered, became quiet and a bit endearing in the face. LJ's mom was melodramatic and threw things—large things—when angered. "Just park on the grass," he said. "Slow down. I'll come—pick you up. We'll talk. What about your book?" He knew that he should talk smoother, use more conjunctions—not be so monotone, so *funereal*. He shouldn't have brought up the book.

"Yeah, talk about my book!" LJ's mom shouted. "When have you ever fucking wanted to talk about my book! Okay. Well then! I'm slowing down. Lewly J. Oh god, what am I doing? I won the lottery, moved to

Florida. What will I *do* tomorrow? What will I do once I'm dead? What will happen to us?"

"It will—" He didn't want to say that it would all be okay, that things would get better. Things would get worse, he knew. There would be old age, cancer, arthritis, global warming, tidal waves, acid rain—life was just a tiny, moonstruck thing, really, and the world was just a small, failed place. "We'll go out," he said. He was bad at optimism, at invigoration, at whatever this was right now. "You, me, Jed. LJ. We'll go to the beach."

"Yeah right!" LJ's mom shouted. "*The beach*," she screamed. "What bullshit! You think you're so nice. Sitting at home or whatever." She paused. She was crying now. "What have you sacrificed? What have you ever done for someone else? Why can't you—"

Jed's dad didn't say anything—he knew she was maybe right, that if he tried hard enough, he *could* love her, and so why didn't he? If you had to try hard in life not to hurt people, not to harm others, didn't you also have to try hard to help people? To love people? Were there limits to this? Some threshold? Could you ever do enough?—and she cried a little and then hung up.

Later that night, she drove onto Jed's dad's yard and fell out of her car. Jed's dad woke up and came outside. She was lying on the grass. She smelled of alcohol and perfume. "This is just a weird dream," she was saying.

"This is all just a weird dream." She was rolling and she rolled onto the sidewalk, scraping herself, and then was stopped by the mailbox. Jed's dad pulled her up and she fell back down. "Dream film doesn't develop in the real world," she shouted. She put her face into the grass.

"Yes it does," Jed's dad said. It seemed to him, then, true—it did develop in the real world, though maybe at a special store. It was 4 a.m.

"It doesn't," she said, a bit wanly. "This is... a weird dream." People had their sprinklers on. The air was a bit misty, and there was a little fog.

"It's not a dream," Jed's dad said. In his periphery, he could see things, vague and kind of buoyily floating about—mailboxes, garbage cans, recycling bins. It was trash night. "This is real," he said. He looked for the moon, but saw only trees—the trees of his yard, other people's yards; the leaves pale and spurned as freshwater shells. Something large had been flying about his face and he now slapped it blindly out of the air; against his open palm it made a tiny noise that stayed in his head, pinging there arhythmically, distortedly loud.

LJ's mom had begun to put grass into her mouth. "I can do anything," she said. "This is just a stupid dream." She passed out, then woke up. She began quietly to cry. She looked up at Jed's dad, opened her mouth, covered her mouth, crawled to a stand, and then ran away. In the morning, her car was still in Jed's dad's yard. The inside of the car was very clean. There was a pink bottle of perfume super-glued to the dashboard. Jed's dad drove it back to her house and walked home. Many of the houses, he noticed, had "For Sale" signs up. Every house, it seemed. One house had been painted a deep, dark, transmogrified green. Another house looked really strange, somehow fundamentally different from all the others. A basketball was rolling down the middle of the street and a boy ran out of a house, picked it up, punted it into someone's side yard. Jed's dad began to run after that. As he ran, everything around his head quaked. He ran home.

School began. Jed was held back in the fourth grade, as planned. He didn't see LJ anymore. She seemed always to be on some kind of fieldtrip. Her fifth-grade teacher encouragd his students to doodle in their textbooks, to talk to their textbooks, to *talk back* to their textbooks. Homework was mostly pun-orientated. One assignment, a fill-in-the-blank type thing, involved Rambo, Rimbaud, and a ram named Bo. "The world has come and gone," LJ's teacher said, quoting his own poetry. "Now is only what is left. A time for leaving, and for cake. The wash and foam of last things, we'll float it out. We'll eat fancy cake. We'll be the wave that goes, and goes, and goes a little more, and then doesn't go anymore." Then he took the class on another fieldtrip.

Nationwide there was, at first, a time of increased lawmaking. Things were generally banned. There was no trust anywhere, and nothing was acceptable. A bill outlawing love was reportedly bring drafted. There was a law that, by accident, outlawed itself. Anything there was had a law for or against it. People, having paid fines for whatever infraction, went home, more inspired than outraged, and wrote their own laws, striving for originality and footnotes. "Laissez-faire," they said stupidly. "Denouement." Other things were said. As more things were said, people became gradually wittier. "Anarchy, apathy, and—" they said. "The three A's."

There was a general drift towards the arbitrary view, the solipsistic and apolitical.

Laws, then, began to be lifted. The drinking age was lowered, then gotten rid of. It became okay to break any of the smaller laws. A large region of the nation acquiesced to some ancient aphorism espousing playfulness. It was shown on TV how you might empty a package of Skittles plus all your prescription pills into a fanny pack and take one mystery pill every four to six hours. People grew amused. Cops covered their helmets and firearms—like guitars—with ironic stickers. "Mitochondria," said the stickers. "Bernoulli's law."

Helicopter pilots, having discovered that they could do tricks, took to the skies in waves, cityward from the suburbs, spinning, diving, circling tall buildings—enacting any scene from any movie. When a mistake in copyediting sent an oil liner to the Galapagos Islands, they left it there, crew and all, calling it innovative—a kind of achievement.

Still, it was not *all* fun and games. That was just the mainstream. More people, actually, were staying home, grim-faced and too well-read. More people were going to bed with a shooting sense of desperation. There were suicides in the night, feral screams from the wall-packed insides of houses. Wolves and bears and other animals, homeless and fed-up, began to use the streets, the sidewalks, the buildings—any kind of infrastructure. Families of possums moved onto front porches, chewed through to living rooms, and cut people off in their own hallways. August, September, many people simply ceased to exist, seemed to be there one day but not the next, but then there they were again, the day after, walking the dog, for an hour, after which they disappeared again, completely—*murdered*, some said, *at last*, as it was annoying, this back and forth of being there, not being there.

TV, though, was booming. It was said that there now more channels than there were people. That when you died, when you *passed on*, it was *into TV*. "TV for president," people muttered, sincerely, at their own flat-faced, blueblazing TVs.

LJ's mom herself no longer watched TV. She bought stuff for LJ—literature, stuffed animals, a typewriter—though LJ was rarely ever home anymore, seemed always to be at school. LJ's mom actually was not doing too good. She had lost it a bit. She had purchased a vacuum cleaner the size of a lawnmower, the idea of which depressed her enormously. She felt constantly *impending*. The daily experience of things thwarted her, like some theory of quantum mechanics she just could not understand. She took to eating candy and became sallow and uninspired in the face, like a curry dish. She bought yet more things. People from far away—from TV, she felt—came daily to her front door, sold her stuff. Nights, she lay awake, waiting for morning, for the sun to come and crash her brightly along, which it would do. She sometimes thought dizzily of packing up, taking a trip, entering into TV... or some other place, any yet unsquandered world, as there must be, she felt, somewhere one could go; that if this world was ruined, if one messed up, there would be another place, sympathetic and conciliatory, to leave towards.

The first day of October, a group of her relatives flew down from Canada—six or seven grown-ups—

and lived with her. She and LJ moved into the house across the street, but more relatives came, friends of relatives, and soon both houses were filled; the day before Halloween, then, they all flew back to Canada, the relatives, the friends—everyone—including, by force of association or by lack of anything else to do, LJ and her mom.

On Halloween Jed sat on the sofa feeling sorry for himself. He had made plans with LJ. They had not seen each other for a long time, and were to trick-or-treat together, and then stay overnight at Jed's house.

Jed began, very quietly, to cry.

Jed's dad had made squid suits for Jed and LJ—they were going to be children giant squid—and Jed, finally, put his on and fell asleep on the sofa, laid across his dad's lap.

In the morning Jed's lung collapsed. It was spontaneous, the nurses said, just happened sometimes—maybe because of stress—and was called pneumothorax, all of which sounded, to Jed's dad, a little absurd, a little *made up*.

A week later, out of the hospital, Jed's lung collapsed again. After that, it happened again. On the third time, they did surgery. Each time, also, they made a slit in Jed's side, between two ribs, held down his body, and forced in a plastic tube, which was connected to a suction machine. The second time, the tube had a point at the end of it—a newer model—and they pushed it in too far, so that it almost pierced through to the other lung. After each chest-tube procedure, Jed would feel lucid, and invulnerable, almost, but also inappreciable, like something momentary and undetectable, and though he wouldn't remember crying, his face would feel hot and wet and open-pored.

Nights, nurses came in with painkillers. Mornings, X-ray machines the size of refrigerators were wheeled in. Jed's dad sat against the wall, straight-backed, below a gray-green window. He watched Jed. The entire time, he had *made up* going through his head, honed and impervious as something to be launched into orbit.

The third time the plastic tube was taken out, the doctor was athletic and did not sit down. He came in the night, cut the sutures, removed the tape. "This'll feel a bit strange," he said. "I'll count to three." Jed feared, as he did each time, that the tube might latch onto something on its way out, that his entire insides—his round and oily heart, his brain somehow—might be yanked out. The doctor said, "One—" then flung his arm back and jerked the tube out from Jed.

After that, everything became a lot less compelling. Things were generally more dispersed, a little vanquished-seeming. Birds flew higher in the air, sometimes flapping straight through to outer space. It was mid-December. Jed began to feel a sort of low-level buzz to his perception of things—a buzz, he felt, that meant he was alive and that everything was real, but just barely—a soft and cellular hum that moved him noticeably along.

LJ's mom phoned Jed's dad one night. She and LJ were back, had bought another house in the same neighborhood.

She invited Jed and his dad over, for Christmas Eve, which was a week away.

On Christmas Eve, Jed and his dad went to LJ's mom's new house. They built a sofa-cushion fort in the living room. There was a giant squid swimming pool float the size of a grown man on top of the TV. LJ's mom had bought it for Jed. A Christmas tree was flashing from another room, lighting up the walls, dark and middleless and fugue'd as some unpeopled dance of the future.

Outside, it was black and silent, as most everyone, it seemed, had by now moved away.

In the living room, blankets and pillows covered the floor. They were all going to sleep there tonight. The TV was on, showing previews. They were to watch the movie *Yi Yi*, by Edward Yang, a favorite of LJ's mom. She was in the kitchen, which was open to the living room. "Cream of broccoli and Swiss cheese," she was saying. "Everyone will love this. It has the most beautiful color. I always thought it was like what you'd see if you were falling through the sky and went on your back. The wind going across, the trees reflected onto the clouds, all creamy and moving around. The sun glowing somewhere…"

Jed's dad was in LJ's room, moving LJ's mattress out into the living room. He was taking his time. He was thinking that maybe he would begin, now, to long for some outlying aspect of LJ's mom, to yearn gradually for her, to work towards a real kind of wanting, and finally, then, some day—some breezy February morning, years from now—look at her face or eyes or neck, at whatever would be the most *her* part of her, and try, with all of slight and glancing life, to love her wholly, truly, and knowingly.

Jed was inside the sofa-cushion fort and so was LJ. They were both ten now. Jed had on his squid suit and LJ had on bunny slippers. "I'd like to disappear one day," LJ's mom was saying, in the kitchen. She talked in a soft, uninflected way, like it was just to herself. "I get the feeling sometimes that I can do that. It's like there's some place I really want to go to, and I'm not sure where, but I can still go. I think I'd really like that. I'd sit down one afternoon. I'd say, 'Okay now, Susan, time to go.' Clasp my hands or something. Then I'd do it. I'd just be gone then. No one would know. I wouldn't even know." Jed and LJ were crawling through the fort, which tunneled around and over the sofa. Jed was anticipating the part where he'd go up, onto the sofa, then over, in a drop, to the carpet. LJ was listening to her bunny slippers shuffling behind her—like real bunnies, she was thinking, baby ones.

That night Jed woke up. He was on the floor, on blankets. He saw in the reflection of the TV that LJ's mom was lying on the sofa, behind him. Her eyes were open. She lay on her side and looked very awake. She looked worried, Jed thought.

She shut her eyes tight and kept them scrunched like that—hard. Then she slowly opened them until they became very wide. She blinked a few times, but kept her eyes large and round, her face a face of surprise. Then she stopped that and looked worried again.

Jed watched her in the TV. He remembered something—his dad and LJ's mom, one night in the front yard; she was on the grass, crying. He had forgotten. He thought of all the time since then—it seemed so long ago—and that LJ's mom was still sad, even now. He pushed his blanket off his body and stood up. His dad and LJ were asleep on the floor. He looked at LJ's mom. Outside, through the sliding glass door, the small, low moon was glowing bright and impressive, like something trying very hard—wanting, maybe, to be a real planet. "You can't sleep?" Jed said. LJ's mom was smiling at him. "Jed," she whispered after a while. "Did you just say something?" She yawned and let her mouth go large and wide and her eyes get watery.

Jed watched that, then lay back down and pulled his blanket over his head, and closed his eyes. From somewhere far away, there was the tired, tortured noise of someone screaming, the human voice of it deadened and decentralized, but there—something of concern and procrastination, wretched and veering and through the throat. Jed felt very awake. His eyes beat lightly against his closed lids. They wouldn't keep still, and as he concentrated on them, as he tried to stop their trembling, he began to feel that he was going to cry. He didn't know why, but he was affected suddenly in this way. He was going to cry. But then he didn't. He felt instead a bit out of breath, felt a kind of anxiety, a quickening, something hollow and neutral moving up through his chest. He felt excited, but in a rushed and terrible way. What he felt, it was less a feeling than a kind of knowledge; it was a subtle knowing, an *almost* knowing, that he was here—that he was once, and now, here—but that he would someday no longer be; and so here he was, then, leaving, all so fast and calm and without a fight, without a *way* to fight, but just this haze of departure, steady and always and all so like a dream, this leaving without having ever *been there*. It was as if he were already gone.

Insomnia for a
Better Tomorrow

First week of February you began to suspect that, for the rest of your life, nothing might happen. This was one of those years. You mail-ordered a special mattress, and napped too much. In restaurants, people ordered the ice-cream cake, shoved their hands under their thighs, and talked loudly about death. On TV, politicians began to snack from Ziploc bags, like a provocation. Almonds, raisins. Sour Patch Kids.

Things, you felt, had changed.

There was a new foreboding to the room in which you slept. There was the fear, now, that all your anxieties and disconsolations might keep on escalating and never stop. There was the theoretical chance that if you threw a banana at a wall the banana might go through the wall.

"Oh well," Brian said. He had begun to order two coffees at once, two different flavors. "Yeah," he said. "I don't care."

His girlfriend Chrissy sat opposite him in a padded chair. They were in a coffee place and there was a table between them. This was Manhattan.

"The key to coffee is to not care anymore," Brian said. "Tolerance and addiction are wrong. They're just wrong. You drink one cup, two cups, ten. Whatever. You keep going. Maybe in the end you're up to fifteen cups, but you always feel good, until you die."

"You're ignoring the financials of it," Chrissy said. She had a muffin and an herbal tea side by side in front of her.

"No I'm not. It's the same," Brian said. "You keep going into debt, buying whatever. You owe a hundred million dollars. Finally you die." He was feeling a bit nauseated today. "You can't argue this," he said.

"By going into debt," Chrissy said. "You're hurting other people."

"Credit card people aren't people," Brian said. "They're credit card people."

Chrissy moved her muffin away from her herbal tea. "You think you're so cool," she said.

Was she being hostile? Brian couldn't tell anymore. Their love had been spent. Brian had spent it. There had been a sale at the mall, and Brian had brought coupons. "Buy things; we'll make her better," the mall had said. Brian had looked around a bit carelessly, without focusing on any one thing, but just making a vague sweep of it all. "Well, okay," he'd said.

"You think you're so wise," Chrissy said. "You think you know more about life than the Dalai Lama or whoever. You secretly think that."

"What?" Brian said. "Stop it. I'm just saying things." He scratched the back of his neck. He looked at the muffin on the table. He began to say something that took a long time to say, but he didn't know what it was, and no one else heard anything of it. His mouth moved, but no sounds came out, which could sometimes happen—you could speak and no sounds would come out.

There was a rumor that year, that you might not be yourself. That you might actually be someone else. One of those people who refuse antidepressants, who can't hold down a job, who ends up sleeping, finally, in a hole.

That might be you, was what the rumor said.

People talked. They said, "There's this rumor...." Then they pointed out something amusing that was happening in the distance. They shrugged. Itched their forearms. They were easily distracted. Later on, though, in the mouthy dens of their bathrooms, they looked in their mirrors, and they just were not sure. *Someone* was there; but was it them? And so they believed. They said things like, "What does it even matter. I might not even be myself." Then they threw themselves off a bridge, or else drank a quart of ice coffee and watched *Indiana Jones and the Temple of Doom.*

One night, after sex, Brian had—instead of making the dash through the kitchen, to the bathroom—cleaned himself with paper towels, rolled over, and gone to sleep. Chrissy had shaken her head at that, had made an annoyed noise and then run through the kitchen and showered.

But soon after, she too began to use paper towels. And then when they ran out of paper towels, they started using toilet paper, and a couple of weeks after that they stopped having sex.

It had become, in too many ways, similar to going to the bathroom.

Now they hugged a lot but rarely kissed. They said things like, "Instead of saying 'good night' every night, let's just assume that we want each other to have a good night. That way we don't have to feel obligated to say it every night." They looked into each other's eyes, and they saw contact lenses—the seized UFOs of them, dumb and shunned as plates. They yawned. They yawned wantonly, without covering their mouths.

They were having a fight one morning in their kitchen, in Brooklyn. Chrissy had spilled orange juice on the floor and then tried to kick it under the refrigerator with her sandals. Brian had watched through the hinge-area of the bedroom door. Had then walked in asking Chrissy if she thought this was a farm. Had kept asking that.

"You're like a cow," Brian said. "Yeah you are. No, a boar. I mean a pig. You think this is a farm."

"Brian," Chrissy said. She tried to look languished and fading-away—something like a corpse sinking into a lake at night—but ended up looking trashy and depraved, like a hooker. "Hey," she said. "You've never given me an orgasm."

"What?" Brian said. "Listen to me. Same here."

"What?"

"I never had an orgasm with you," Brian said.

"You Brian—you idiot, I mean. I've seen evidence of it."

"You believe everything you see? It's my body and I'm telling you that I didn't ever orgasm with you." Brian turned and opened the refrigerator and stuck his head in.

"Fuck you," Chrissy said. "Yeah you did." At this point in their relationship, it was overridingly important to win all arguments. Things were somehow at stake. Chrissy picked up Brian's shoes. "Look at me," she said. "Hey. Come here." She went to the window and opened it, held the shoes outside. Brian looked. His head had begun to hurt. "Admit it," Chrissy said. "Or I'm dropping your shoes."

"I don't lie," Brian said.

"I'm dropping your shoes."

"Are you going to drop them," Brian said. "Or just talk about dropping them?"

"No I'm not. I'm not that kind of person. What if I hit someone's head? See, you don't even know me."

"You think *you* know you?" Brian said. "Chrissy, you might not even be yourself. Remember that homeless woman you wouldn't give money to? Yeah, I saw that. Well you might be her. So fuck you." He put his head back in the refrigerator, and grinned. Sometimes you had to be a little bit insane. You had to say, "Give me that. Let me do it." You had to take things from the world and bend them and then put them back in the world, bent like that.

It had something to do with fear. You had to reverse things. Make the world afraid of you.

Chrissy moved home to the Midwest. They had lived previously in her apartment, paid for by her parents, and Brian now moved to Jersey City, which was the other Brooklyn.

He used his college degree and got a job at a magazine corporation.

There were rooms with desks and rooms with views, and they gave Brian a room with a desk. "All the rooms have desks," they said. "It's a joke. So keep your pants on. It's all a joke. Everything. You, me, this room. This whole damn spinning-swaying, car-crashing world."

That was the tone of the place.

Each morning, a girl named Jennika would enter Brian's room with a list of tasks.

"Here's your tasks for today, Brian," she would say.

Brian soon developed a crush on Jennika. She had a face, had all the right angles. She was shy and intelligent. Or else conceited and slow. Still, they could be happy together, Brian guessed, if she were only willing.

"That's a strange name," Brian said one morning.

"Oh." Jennika hesitated, then smiled. "Here are your tasks."

"You usually say, 'Here's your tasks for today, Brian,'" Brian said. He sometimes had the feeling that he was doing something illegal, something that he might be incarcerated for; or else something illusory, something that produced results, but only in some other, parallel universe, something that, in this universe, just did not produce any results.

"I do. Yeah." Jennika blushed. She turned to leave.

"Wait," Brian said. "What does this company do exactly? What do we make?" He had been wondering. Had come to one conclusion that they were producing a magazine for robots—because robots, Brian knew, would one day conquer the world. Afterwards they would probably want to read magazines.

"We're a magazine corporation," Jennika said. A kind of gluey indecision began in her eyes, a slow and brainward strain—this sort of melancholy distortion. It made it seem like she was very uncomfortable being alive.

"Jennika is a good name." Brian tried to keep his eyes very wide and friendly, but could feel that the rest of his face was changing. Maybe the strain was in his eyes and not Jennika's. Moments like these, it was hard to distinguish between yourself and others.

Jennika started to say something. She stopped. Her face became a little grotesque, but she didn't turn to leave. They looked at each other. There was a long silence. That kind of silence that keeps going, that you then resign yourself to—like taking a step, and your foot going down, going further, not touching floor, your face falling, your thoughts going, "The ground, where's the ground, oh well, oh well…"

They didn't talk to each other anymore after that.

After work, Brian would spend a lot of time—too much, he suspected—going around looking for a place to eat. It would often take up the entire night, like some kind of wan and moony quest, something shameful and cheaply existential. He would inevitably be unsatisfied, would regret not eating whatever other food—that eluding food of otherness.

In his apartment he would lie on his bed and allow himself some fantasies, which led mostly to masturbation, though it would also lead to list making—to brief, abstract moments when he would understand that he needed simply to do things and then his life would be changed.

Sometimes, unwilling to sleep into the sameness of tomorrow, he would shower and then go out into the night, hoping to fall in love, to be whisked away into that sort of a life. He would buy fey candies, and a sugary drink. When a car came by, he would fear a drive-by shooting or kidnapping. He stayed close to the street-lamps. To discourage hoodlums—there were hoodlums in this neighborhood, it was said—he walked slantly and often turned to cross the street eccentrically.

It was a little thrilling.

Eventually, though, he would become tired and disenchanted. He would go back to his room and feel as if an entire month was inside of him. He would feel big and emptied like that. He would have a stomachache. Nothing was going to happen tonight, or ever. He would shower. Brush his teeth. Lie on his bed, and go into a flat and perished kind of sleep, one in which all his dreams were fraught and blotched and melodramatic and loud, like watching a movie from the front row.

He began to doubt his ability to make friends. He began, as maybe a kind of detachment—or maybe a kind of antisocial sarcasm—to take things literally. What materials did one need in order to make a friend? Was this mostly a DIY thing, or could you pay someone else to do it for you, diligently and in one night, while you slept? He sometimes brought a second mirror into the bathroom and looked at his face from different angles. Was he ugly? How ugly?

He lay in bed, remembering past things from his life.

As a teenager, he made screaming noises at night in his room, like a deranged person. He threw his electrical pencil sharpener at the walls. His mother was downstairs in bed, crying a little, mostly asleep. Brian, in his room, felt as if he might explode, might already—in a slow and miniscule and lingering way—be exploding. He needed to explode. He lay there motionless, but he also lay there exploding. He smooshed his head into his mattress, making sounds like, "aaaghh," and "ngggg," and then went downstairs. He stood in the doorway of his mother's bedroom. He started yelling things. His mother woke, warm and puffy from sleep, and—after Brian finished yelling—whispered that she was sorry for being a bad mother. Her face, ensconced in hair and pillow, was dramatic and friendless as something cocooning. She looked like a little girl, and Brian stood there, taking this in—trying to get at the meaning of things, to fit at once into his mind all the false and watery moments of his life. He stood there, and he looked. He looked some more. And then he went back to his room. He wrote down on paper: "Don't hurt anyone again."

But he did. He went on blaming his mother. Yelling at her. About how he couldn't make friends, how it was because she spoiled him, didn't ever punish him, didn't put him into uncomfortable situations, didn't socialize him, etc.

"Don't hurt anyone again."

Brian had a little stack of those papers somewhere.

And, finally, he had, recently, begun to do less of this hurting of other people, this blaming of others, of his mother. Though it was mostly because he did not see anyone anymore. Probably that was the reason.

At work, he stopped saying hi to people, unless they said hi to him first, at which he would then say hi eagerly back and try to smile. But he was not good at smiling. That ataxic struggle of the mouth, it sometimes felt to Brian like a kind of snarling. He could see it on other people's faces, that he was not smiling, but probably snarling.

After a while, people stopped saying hi to him.

The work atmosphere became foretoken and noir, like a Batman movie.

Most days now Brian didn't say anything out loud.

He took to sitting in parks. Observing people. Sometimes he would see a girl and a boy holding hands and it would make him happy. "How nice," he would think. "How nice it is for them." Though most of the time it just made him jealous. He imagined the couples coming up to him and patting his hair, slapping his cheeks, like a baby. Laughing into his face. He would *dare them* to.

He bought encrusted nuts from the "Nuts 4 Nuts" people, who were nice people, if a little doomed-seeming.

He made it a point to say thank you and goodbye whenever buying food or other items.

Have a good day. Goodnight.

One day he didn't go to work.

And then it became so difficult and useless to go to work that he stopped going.

There were moments when you knew for sure that you would never be happy. You thought, "Nothing's going to happen this year. Ten years, sixty years. That's right. Of course." And you felt all those years, there, inside of you, wandering the institutional corridors of your bones, playing ping-pong in the unkempt game-room of your heart, not keeping score, not even using the paddles—but playing stupidly a kind of handball-table hockey. But not even doing that, really. Just standing around. All the years, just standing there. Waiting to happen.

You thought, "Well, then..."

And you imagined being dead. You imagined it might be something like a gasp. A normal gasp, but sustained, and forever—and maybe outside of you, sucking at your air, the suffocation and discomfort increasing without end. The mouth-faced animal of death—flying, taking, wanting always more, like something intelligent and sane, but delinquent and two-years-old. The mouth-headed gliding lung of death. "Of course," you thought. Because these things were possible. They were. There was even a thing called anti-matter, Brian knew. And black-matter, which was invisible. Eighty to eighty-five percent of all matter was actually black-matter. Brian had read that in a book. There had been an enormous question mark on the opposite page.

For a long time, there was the sensation of life becoming smaller.

Life lost gradually the things of itself. The peripheral items wandered amnesically off, and then flew away, not amnesic at all, just too optimistic and quixotic to stay. You became meeker and less opinionated through all the small maintenances of yourself—the self-aware, mid-day toothbrushing, the splashless handwashing. And the one eye of your soul—the angrysad Cyclops of your soul, with its spiked club, its dark and forsaken cave, its island routine—began to squint, to slowly close.

Life became a puny, disassembling thing.

Something that needn't be paid any attention to—that you could just leave there.

Brian found that he did not need much to get through each day. Decent Chinese food, a Jean Rhys novel, iced coffee. That was enough for one day. It helped if he stayed in his room and slept more than 14 hours a day, which he did; the peculiar, detached success of being in bed—it was like the padded practice of a thing before the real hurt and triumph of the actual thing.

His fantasies became less masturbatory and more about time-travel and childhood.

He grew content in a leveled and agrarian way, like a grass.

Still, though, once, unable to sleep, he had, in one dilapidated night, allowed himself to search out an adult store and buy two porno magazines and some other items. He read them front to back, stopping carefully for the photos. Later, he looked in his bathroom mirror, pointed at his reflection, and said, "Born alone, die alone." He was giddy with shame and despair after that. Then he wasn't giddy anymore, and he went to sleep. When he woke, it was night again. He wrapped the pornography and the other items in three plastic grocery bags, tied it up, put it in a Mercer Street Used Books bag, tied that up, carried it six blocks in a direction he hadn't been before, and shoved it in someone's trashcan.

It was important, he knew, not to become one of those irrecoverable persons.

One day he was looking out his window, staring at people who were climbing onto each other's backsides laughing—and he began to think that if he got a job, he could meet people. He seemed to realize this. He needed a job. He needed also to join clubs. Water polo, yoga. Bowling.

In Manhattan, he had a coffee.

He walked up Sixth Avenue. He turned toward Union Square. The streets seemed to have recently been blasted clean. "Nice job," Brian thought. He was impressed. He felt good. He went through the park, looking and smirking—not in an unfriendly way—at people, and continued uptown.

Around 33rd street there was a strip club or something. It had a sexy-lady sticker on the door. It said, "Live Girls." Brian thought of maybe going in. Maybe not, though. He would no doubt affect gauntness, perversity, desperation, and condescension. The other patrons would somehow affect virtue and dignity, a kind of Nordic diplomacy. They would be enterprising and pressed for time.

Brian walked into Times Square.

There was a Brazilian steak place here that he liked. He used to go all the time with Chrissy.

He walked back downtown. He didn't feel at all good anymore. "Because of the coffee," he thought. The caffeine was no longer doing what it would do. He sat in Washington Square Park. He had never liked Chrissy, he guessed. Had never really liked anyone, probably. "That's it," he thought. His shoulders and neck were cramped from trying too hard for good posture, which he knew was important for confidence, bones, self-esteem, mood, attractiveness, etc. A young man wanted to sell Brian some drugs. Brian shook his head, and looked at the ground. The young man stayed to talk. He sat. He made some distinctions between psychologists and psychiatrists, and then complimented Brian's teeth. "He says that to everyone," Brian thought. Next, your teeth would be pulverized to a fine powder. "Thank you," Brian said, and the young man left.

It had become very dark outside.

Brian stood and walked in some vague direction, into a bookstore.

He moved himself around the aisles. He tried not to look too lonely. He opened a book but could not concentrate. Everyone else, he felt, was on a choicer plane of existence. They all seemed very confident that the world was a good and auspicious place. Brian's face had gone hot and severe. The clam-meat of his face. People could see. His neck tremored a little. That kind of inchoate weeping that would always happen to him if he stayed in public too long, it happened now.

"This is… unreasonable," he thought.

He bought and ate a cookie the size of his hand. He felt like vomiting. He went out into the city. It seemed louder than before. Trucks the size of small buildings were coming consecutively down the street. A team of men were jackhammering the street. There was a group of drunken people with glossy heads.

Brian walked slowly around, then came to a stop. His mind went blank. Time moved around him, like a crowd. "Walk," he thought. "Move, go…."

He thought that he would see a movie, then.

He bought a ticket for 12:45 a.m. at the Union Square Theatre. He had one hour. He walked in a direction, but saw an acquaintance across the street and turned and walked in another direction.

From a deli, he bought a 16 oz. beer and a soy drink that was also a tea drink.

Outside, he made sure to look far into the distance. If an acquaintance confronted him, started questioning him, he would have no choice but to run away. He sat in a dark area of Union Square Park.

He drank his tea drink.

He looked absently at the label. "2000% Vitamin C," it said.

In the movie theatre there were a few other solitary people. Some had a kind of space-time enlightened gaze, a beatific vacancy about their eyes that made them look very confident, but in a bionic way, as if they were truly—scientifically—simultaneously in the future, at home, eating something with a large spoon. The others, including Brian, blinked a lot. After each blink their focus would be on a different area outside of their heads. They looked as if under attack, which was because they felt as if under attack.

Brian went into the bathroom and stood in a stall.

He locked the door. He took his beer out of his bag, looked at his beer, put his beer back in his bag. He stood there until a few minutes past the start-time of the movie. He splashed water to his face, left the bathroom, went in the theatre, and sat in the back row.

After a while, he took his beer out of his bag and opened it. The beer said, "Kuhchshhh." It was tall, silvery, and cold. On the screen, a beautiful girl who was

Natalie Portman was taking an aggressive interest in a depressed, monotone man whose mother had recently passed away.

Brian almost shouted, "Bullshit," but was able to control himself.

"My hair is blowing in the wind," said Natalie Portman, whose name was Sam.

Brian began to think, "If I were as beautiful as her..." He stopped himself and drank his beer. His face soon became warm. There was an asphyxiative pleasure to it, like a kind of choking or crying. His heart was beating fast. The movie was wide and calm on the screen. Cool air was coming down. Brian leaned back into his seat and put his feet up. There were moments when you were not afraid of anything anymore. These moments it became clear that all things were arbitrary, that everything was just made of atoms, or whatever, and therefore everything was, firstly, one same, connected thing, a kind of amorphous mass wherein areas of consciousness moved from place to same place—or maybe did not even move, but, because all places were the same, were just *there*. Guilt, fear, meaning, love, loneliness, death. These words, you realized, were all the same. Everything was all the same. There was what there was, and that was what all there was; there was you, and you were everything. These moments would last seconds, minutes, or maybe an hour, and they were euphoric. They could happen from reading, looking at a painting, from music—from any kind of art, really, or from witnessing or experiencing something startling or strange; but never from other people. These moments you could almost cry. Life was simply, obviously, and beautifully meaningless.

Brian in the theatre that night, drinking beer, felt this.

These moments would end, though, when you realized that all that amorphous mass stuff was, well—bullshit. Was good on paper, maybe, but in real life was impossible. Unlivable. Something only a philosopher, a paid one—a philosopher that received cash for what he or she did—would benefit from. Things weren't connected. Not really. You were one person alive and your brain was encased inside a skull. There were other people out there. It took an effort to be connected. Some people were better at this than others. Some people were bad at it. Some people were so bad at it that they gave up.

Sasquatch

Though she'd begun to get a bit fat that winter, it was in February, around when her father found a toy poodle (sitting there, in the side yard, watchful and expectant as a person), and adopted it, that a weightlessness entered into Chelsea's blood—an inside ventilation, like a bacteria of ghosts—and it was sometime in the fall, before her 23rd birthday, that her heart, her small and weary core, neglected now for years, vanished a little, from the center out, took on the strange and hollowed heaviness of a weakly inflated balloon.

This wasn't sadness—there were no feelings of desperation or disaster, nothing like depression with its one slowed-down realization of having been badly and untraceably misunderstood—but rather a plain, artless form of loneliness; something uninteresting, factual, and teachable, perhaps, to children or adults, with flashcards of household items (toothbrush, pillow), coloring books of fleeting, unaccompanied things (hailstones that melt midair; puddles formed and unseen and gone; illusions of friends in the periphery), and a few real-world assignments (post-nap trip to the pet store in the early, breezy evening; Halloween night asleep on the sofa; Saturday night dinner in the parking lot, looking through the windshield at the pizza buffet restaurant you just got take-out from).

"I don't want to serve those guys," Chelsea said at Denny's to her manager Bernadette. "You do it please?" Around a person like Bernadette, who once said to a plate of pancakes she was going to fire it, then went around telling everyone, including patrons, about that— "I fired some pancakes earlier, so watch out"—Chelsea could get pleading and playful a bit; around most other people she just felt surreally retarded or else profoundly insane all the time.

TAO LIN

"I'm going to fire you," Bernadette said. "Wait. I'm going to promote you."

"Then I can fire myself," Chelsea said. "Yeah. I'll just fire myself." She'd get a job wearing a hot dog suit, roadside—dancing, losing weight, holding up a vaguely controversial sign: *Juicy, tender, cheap; so eat me.* Teenagers would drive by and assault her. "But yeah; they went to high school with me. But we pretended no one knew each other. They wouldn't look at me. Even them two pretended they didn't know each other. That's how bad it got."

"You take big head, then. The big-headed guy. I'll do the losers you went to high school with."

"I hate it when people call people losers," Chelsea said.

"Look at me. I manage a chain restaurant that sells pancakes at night. I tell my boyfriend he's a loser every day. I did that today. Who wants to succeed in life? No one."

"Um, I'm a waitress at Denny's, and you're my manager. And you're like one year older than me, and way more successful." Though she knew while saying it that it wasn't going to make much sense, she said it anyway, with a sort of conviction, even, because she was not good at functioning in real-time, especially when distracted, like she was now, by how tiny and beautiful Bernadette was, like a child, almost, whereas Chelsea herself was homelier, medium-sized, and, in an obscure way that she sometimes—usually after coffee—thought, but never really believed, might be mysterious and therefore attractive, disproportioned, like a vitamin-deficient, softly-mutated, childlike sort of adult. "Why are you calling that guy 'big head'?" she said.

Bernadette moved toward Chelsea—who, as always, when approached, began like a blowfish to feel growing and more sensitive—and hugged her. "Calm down, girl," Bernadette said, and something behind Chelsea's ribs that had been swinging, black and heavy like a pendulum, swung a little more, then detached and fell away, and in the unoccupied moment that followed—it was one of those moments you could go away from and relax a little and then come back as how you yourself wanted to be, rather than what the world wanted you to be—Chelsea had the thought that Bernadette was a good person, and felt like she might cry, or at least say something. But Bernadette stepped back and Chelsea hesitated, then went to the big-headed man and looked at him, the secret reality of his skull, thinking that if it wasn't so large he would've made more friends as a child, wouldn't now be eating alone on a Friday night.

TAO LIN

She took his order, wandered around—always felt like she was 'wandering around,' even at work, which seemed wrong in some deep-brained way—served him, and, while seating an elderly couple, then, watched as her old high school classmates left without paying.

"Hey," she said in back to Bernadette. "Those high school guys just ditched."

Bernadette filled a soft drink and set it down. "Chase them," she said. "Now's your chance to scream at them. I'm serious. It's an opportunity." She pushed Chelsea toward the entrance, and Chelsea went there. "Call them names! It'll feel good."

Outside, they were across the parking lot, getting into a car, and Chelsea chased after them—vaguely, in a jog. She felt tired, but wanted to scream things. Maybe she should call them shitheads. She kind of wanted to wave at them. The air was warm and things were quiet, and she didn't want to run anymore, but they'd think she was strange if she just stood there with a blank face—they'd say she stopped because of being too fat. She ran at the car and one of them put his head out a window and screamed something. His voice cracked. His mouth stayed open a moment and Chelsea looked for teeth, but there was just black space there, a hole on the face.

Back in Denny's, Bernadette said she'd pay.

"I'll pay," Chelsea said. "They think I pretended I didn't know them."

"What are you talking about? I'll pay."

"Fine," Chelsea said. "You pay."

"I'll pay half. But tell me where they live and we'll vandalize their homes."

"I don't know them."

"We'll bury their mailbox in the neighbor's yard," Bernadette said. "This'll be good. Causing destruction when it's justified is good." Chelsea's mother left when Chelsea was in middle school. She had written a note, then one morning was standing by her car. She hadn't ever smiled, really—they'd been a family of grinners and smirkers—but she did, that day, in the driveway, teeth white and glistening as something that in darkness would glow, and it made Chelsea, at the front doorway, smile, too; and she looked up and her dad was also smiling; and her mother drove away. It wasn't so sad (except maybe in the way that all things are sad), as the three of them had never been close, but just mumbling and monosyllabic all the time, like an inwardly preoccupied people, distracted always by their own supposed aliveness—how their wet hearts, placed there, behind the breezy hollows of the lungs, in the saunaish chest, warm and pressurized as a yawn, would sometimes (at night or in the afternoons, though sometimes over a few weeks, or seasons, even) feel tired and too hot, and then airy, and dry, and finally a little floating and skyward, as if wanting to leave, having realized, perhaps, wrongly or not, that life was elsewhere; or, rather, that their service was not to these lives, not to these single people, but to some history of people, already gone, faceless and sadder as some ocean in some night somewhere, not touching anything, or existing, even, but feelable, still, sometimes, cold and temperatureless, like a sudden awareness of time, of being actually alive; a sensation of falseness, really, of being lied to.

"You should be a bounty hunter, or something," Chelsea said. "I don't know." In high school she got nervous around people, and spent too much time on the Internet. She began to stutter a little, and one Christmas her dad—who was a card-giver; had never bought Chelsea, or anyone, a present—ordered her tapes for social anxiety disorder and put them in her room. You were supposed to listen to them and do the assignments and become more outgoing and less afraid. Chelsea cried when she saw them. They didn't talk about it. And though Chelsea listened carefully to all twenty tapes, and tried hard—making small talk with strangers, walking around in malls and making eye-contact with people, calling stores to practice her voice—nothing really changed, and she went to college in New York City, where sometimes, in bed and unsleepy, the rest of her life would quickly assemble and disassemble, as if some faraway eye had glimpsed the entire idea of her, by accident, and had not noticed, really, but subconsciously dismissed it, as an optical illusion; and where, most days, a keen, gray energy (this deadened sort of voltage—something of faux-sophistication, low-grade restlessness, and, in that she often had the urge to stop walking and curl against a building and sleep there and freeze to death, a passive-aggressive sort of suicidal despair) would move through her (though some afternoons around her, uncertainly, like she might be in the way, and then she'd just feel indistinct and hungry).

"We'll chalk their driveways," Bernadette said. "We'll write, 'I am inside your house and will kill you.' Then draw a ghoul. I'd freak out so bad." She laughed. "We did stuff like that in high school. I miss it."

After college, with her higher-education unassimilated and separate and dully stimulating as tropical fish—darting, slowing, and then not floating to the top but just sort of self-destructing—in the light-reflecting pond of her mind, Chelsea returned home to Florida, sat around the house for about a year (eating things, mostly), and, as a way to get out more and maybe make some friends, then, got a job at Denny's.

That was in November, and now it was March, and Chelsea—the water of her mind lately fishless and still, though occasionally something enormous and blurry like the Loch Ness Monster would roll through, in a sort of cartwheel—still got nervous at work, most days had to sit in her car, breathing deep, from the stomach (little towels of air, warm and wrapping against the heart), before going in. But she was glad to have some social interaction, so as not to lose herself completely, as one could do that, she knew, could toss one's life in a pile, like a nail clipper, with a lot of other stuff. It could get thrown out, by accident. And then you had to get a new one. But it wasn't as good. Or maybe it was better— maybe sometimes it was better—so good you couldn't remember the old one anymore.

After work, Chelsea didn't want to go home, and called her dad. "I'm going to Wal-Mart first," she said. "I might try on clothes." A hat. Maybe there'd be a nice hat. "I might go to the bookstore too. So don't worry."

Her dad said he found a white dog. He said something about the stock market, and to buy a movie for him.

In Wal-Mart, the lights were bright and everywhere like in a surgical ward, though also cheap and paneled and vaguely irradiating like in an elementary school or

TV UFO. Chelsea felt disembodied and wandered deep into the clothing section, then went back to her car, and then back in Wal-Mart, to the side of the store not the clothing section, where she found a discount bin, leaned over it—kind of wanting to climb in, like a kid—searched a while, and found a foreign movie she'd seen before, in college. She had downloaded it one night in her dorm room and watched it off her computer screen. It was about a man who suffered from existential despair. He suffered and suffered, and then someone shot him twice in the chest.

"This is a movie to watch on Halloween when the kids are out trick-or-treating," said the register person, an old lady.

"Oh," Chelsea said. "Why?"

"The film's on sale," said the old lady.

"It is?"

"First nothing's on sale. Then five things. Then everything is free."

"Oh," Chelsea said, and almost said, "Cool," as she had a thing—back in college, mostly—where she'd say, "Oh," wait a moment, say, "Cool," and then grin self-consciously. It was her way of saying, "I have no idea how to respond to what you just said. *I* have no idea, but other people, I'm sure, do. It's my fault, not yours. I know I seem disinterested, or something. You shouldn't trust that. I just didn't know how to react. The grin means I'm amiable."

In the parking lot, she drove and parked in a dark area with no other cars around. She reclined her seat, and listened to music. Outside there were trees, a ditch, a bridge, another parking lot. It was very dark. Maybe the Sasquatch would run out from the woods. Chelsea wouldn't be afraid. She would calmly watch the Sasquatch jog into the ditch then out, hairy and strong and mysterious—to be so large yet so unknown; how could one cope except by running?—smash through some bushes, and sprint, perhaps, behind Wal-Mart, leaping over a shopping cart and barking. Did the Sasquatch bark? It used to alarm Chelsea that this might be all there was to her life, these hours alone each day and night—thinking things and not sharing them and then forgetting. The possibility of that would shock her a bit, trickily, like a three-part realization: that there was a bad idea out there; that that bad idea wasn't out there, but here; and that she herself was that bad idea. But recently, and now, in her car, she just felt calm and perceiving, and a little consoled, even, by the sad idea of her own life, as if it were someone else's, already happened, in some other world, placed now in the core of her, like a pillow that was an entire life, of which when she felt exhausted by aloneness she could crumple and

fall towards, like a little bed, something she could pretend, and believe, even (truly and unironically believe;
why not?), was a real thing that had come from far
away, through a place of no people, a place of people,
and another place of no people, as a gift, for no occa-
sion, but just because she needed, or perhaps deserved—
did the world try in that way? to make things fair?—it.

In the morning she looked puffy to herself in the
mirror—not like a person at all, not like anything—and
didn't want to leave the house. She called in sick, went
back to sleep, and woke in the afternoon. She washed
her face, not looking at it, and went into the living
room. Her dad was lying on the carpet, head propped
up, watching the movie she'd bought him. A dog was
walking around. It looked nervous and very small.
Chelsea sat on the sofa and lay down and fell asleep,
and then her dad was touching her shoulder and grinning. "I'm watching it again," he was saying. "The
movie made me feel good. I think I'll watch it again."
The dog was barking somewhere and, in the vague panic
and quicker learning of having just woken up, the world
seemed obscure in a meticulous and exciting way, like in
childhood, perhaps, and the feeling of that glided in,
from some corner of the room, and filled the space in
Chelsea from where once it had left. She was not really
awake; or maybe was still asleep. She didn't know. But

she felt ready (for what, she couldn't tell; just a kind of readiness), and was thinking that there were three of them, like a team or triangle, set to leave this place, safe because of the variety (man, animal, girl) and purposed because of the movie, and, liking the way she felt, then, smiled a little—prepared to travel, or whatever, to some unique and distractionless spot, thinking strange and illogical thoughts, and about to shrink into herself, to fit the small room of being asleep, the boxing-in and cardboard of it, like a shipment that stays, or a heart that goes, into a lung, and sits there, beating into itself, worldless and full.

In the spring, a few months after Chelsea's high school classmates ran out on their check, Bernadette began to talk again about vandalizing them—"We should paint their windows black and superglue their front door"— and Chelsea looked forward to that. But after a while Bernadette stopped talking about it, then one night said she was moving to Seattle with her boyfriend, and a week later was gone. Chelsea was moved to the morning shift—her new manager was balding, with two sons at the community college—and found herself not knowing what to do each day after work. Sometimes she just drove around and listened to the radio. Then she began to sit in her room and go through all her old things, and found her social anxiety tapes, and listened to them, more out of boredom—or nostalgia, even, as sometimes she missed her teenage emotions, those moments when, alone, in her room, in the morning or at night, something in her would deepen, there would be a space and a rush, like a falls, and she would drop a little, into that depth, the secret lake of it, close and warm and wild as, she imagined, a best friend—than in an attempt to change (though of course there was a little hope; always, there was a little hope), but most days just fell asleep, anyway, before each half-hour tape ended, and so after a while just took to taking naps, naturally, without any tapes. One afternoon she had a dream. She and a boy were holding hands on a bus. It was a field trip. In the parking lot there were midgets, talking to her. The boy was in the distance, tall and shy and waiting, and she felt compassionate. She petted the midget's heads, then tentatively picked up two of them—one in each arm—and grinned at the boy, who had a video camera and was filming the movie. She had an idea and hesitated, and picked up a third midget by having her two midgets pick up another midget.

At night, the boy held her and they watched their movie in the Sunshine cinema in Manhattan.

"That was risky," she said in the boy's ear. "The third midget."

"You're risky," he said.

"I like midgets."

"I like you," he said.

And she felt vivid and nervous, and happy.

Another day, a little bored after a nap, she sort of wandered into a strip mall pet-store and—in a tic of expendable income and misdirected loneliness—bought a 50-gallon fish aquarium, with an oak stand. At home, her dad put the poodle, who he'd named Wong Kar-Wai, in the aquarium, and Wong Kar-Wai lay down, unsurprised and accepting; when Chelsea went to take him out, though, she fell and knocked the aquarium off its stand and Wong Kar-Wai landed badly, and yelped, then walked around strangely, as if paralyzed a little; but after a while walked normally and then one day ran away. Chelsea's dad put flyers in people's mailboxes, and an old man called, said he'd found a toy poodle, but that it was his—he lived four houses down, he said, and had almost forgotten about Ronnie, who'd disappeared about half a year ago—and then it was summer and the heat and humidity made Chelsea's skin oily and, for a few days in July, and then an entire week in August, she thought about moving to San Francisco. She felt excited. But she didn't know what she would do there. Probably just work at another Denny's. She wouldn't have any friends—not that she had any now—and her

dad would be alone. And she had to take care of her
fish; she had a lot now. So she decided to stay, and settled into a sort of routine: working, napping, reading,
taking care of her fish, and, on the weekends, eating dinner or seeing movies with her dad, who she more and
more felt comfortable talking to, and who, one evening
in October, then, came home from a walk and said he'd
met a young man, who'd just moved here for graduate
school and with whom he'd set up a date with Chelsea,
and Chelsea went on it, but, driving around—she'd said
something about these two parks she liked, and then
he'd wanted to see them both—was so nervous and
became so silent and still, like a statue, almost, though
also trembling a bit, and sweating, that, finally, after
twenty-five minutes of driving, stupidly, from one park
to the other (the parks were in different counties), staring at things, the young man, who had blonde eyebrows
and had mentioned when he first got in the car that he
felt great, said he felt really sick and needed to go home
and sleep. Chelsea dropped him off, and ate pizza alone
in her car. And felt so disappointed at herself that when
she came home and her dad stood up, smiling, and
asked her how it went, she thought she was going to hug
him and cry, that it would be one of those scenes—like
on TV, when dads say, "Now, now, hey, now," while
holding their daughters, who sob, then sniffle, then eat

TAO LIN

too many cookies and grin—but nothing like that had ever happened to her and she knew it wouldn't now, or probably ever. She said she was sleepy and went to her room, and stood there, in the middle of it, wanting to sleep immediately but knowing she should wash her face and brush her teeth first; and being annoyed at that, and then at everything, at all of canceled and envisioning life, the darkened yearning of upkeep and practice, the sarcasm of it all, like a lie that says it's the truth and begins and goes for a while and then stops being sarcastic and doesn't go anymore, so that when her dad surprised her, a few minutes later, by coming into her room without knocking, catching her just standing there, not doing anything, with the lights off, she got angry, though mostly it was just dismay—a dry and lifeward sort of beating, unpulsing and everywhere as a sky; how could one cope with that?—and looked at her dad, something wild and extrasensory in her eyes, and shouted that he should knock, that he should go away and knock next time. He left and she showered, then wrote a note of apology and found him in the living room, on the sofa, and handed it to him. But at Sweet Tomatoes the next afternoon—a late lunch before an early movie—he didn't ask about the young man, whose name was Mitchell, and she didn't talk about him, and the knowledge of that stayed between them, like a thing that was large and trembled when approached, and they talked less, and the friendliness they'd built between them the past couple of months, like a sandcastle, was subsumed by the water of the last 22 years. In bed that night it felt to Chelsea like whatever this was would go on forever, but also just a little longer, as it was a kind of forever that was so fast and small that it blurred and seemed to be over, already, and always—to be over forever.

And then later that same week at the grocery she saw her manager and turned to go the other direction. She stepped into an instant noodle stand, knocking a few of them down, and began to walk quickly out of the aisle, but then realized that she'd see her manager the next day, at work, and so turned back. He was about twenty feet away and looking at her, and she waved.

"Chelsea," he said.

"Hi," Chelsea said. "I'm just here—for buying some things." He looked a little bored, or else tired, and he gazed at her, a bit meanly, without smiling. She was holding a plum and a toothbrush. She'd been driving around, feeling a little empty, and had wanted a plum, and then had decided to buy a new toothbrush. "Okay," she said. "I'm going to buy this—fruit." Her face was red, and she stuttered a little—something that hadn't happened since high school, she knew immediately.

In the car, she thought about how she'd wanted to go to San Francisco. No one knew because she hadn't told anyone. She thought about some other things—her dad and mom and Bernadette; college and childhood; how when you were two-years old you didn't know what a friend was, but mostly just observed things, without any sadness, and didn't feel alone, even when you were—and then wanted to cry; but it wasn't happening, so she sort of forced herself to, and it worked. She cried a little, then stopped and ate her plum, slowly, in a daze of chewing and swallowing, and then took her new toothbrush out of its packaging and looked at it and put it in her pocket, and after that cried for a longer time and loudly, shaking a bit.

Before going home, she drove around a while—singing along to songs, not thinking anything at all, and with the windows down, to let the wind at her face—so that her dad wouldn't see that she had been crying. In the garage, sitting in the car, she laughed a little, thinking of what she'd said to her manager, then felt nervous and afraid, anticipating when she'd see him again, but the next day he was kind and approached her first, smiling and with a small bag of plums, of which Chelsea, on her break and then after work, ate the entire thing of, as she didn't want to have to explain all this to her dad, or else bring the plums home and have her dad not say anything about them—she didn't want that either.

In December, for her 23rd birthday, Chelsea went bowling with her dad. It was a strange, woozy night, both of them trying for enthusiasm, but trying halfheartedly, or else too hard, or perhaps not even trying anymore—when did *trying* try too hard and escape itself and fly away, leaving you there, below and shrinking?—and ended up with a low-level, unwanted sort of sarcasm; the kind where you smirked a lot.

There was an arcade there, and first thing, before bowling—before bowling two games and stopping for ice cream on the way home (Chelsea's dad insisting on buying a cone and bringing it back to the car, as a sort of surprise, as he felt bad for not getting Chelsea a real present but just a card with money in it; and Chelsea, waiting in the car, looking through the windshield, at her dad in the store looking down through glass, at all the bright and oozy ice creams, to choose something for his daughter, for herself, and feeling, then, in the bones of her face and the dusk of her chest a chill of something casual and temperatureless)—before all that,

Chelsea's dad saw the arcade and went in there and beat a teenager in a fighting game.

"That's not right," the teenager said. "You were lucky. Rematch."

"Good job," Chelsea said. There was something dark and tall in the far corner, past a few billiards tables, and she glanced at it.

"Skill," said Chelsea's dad.

The teenager had a hand in his pocket, low and feeling for quarters, and he looked at Chelsea, and Chelsea looked down at the teenager's shoes—they were green—then elsewhere, and then made eye contact with her dad, by accident, and looked away. But he'd been watching her, so Chelsea looked back; he was grinning, and she felt sorry for him, for having created her—for having brought such a shy and cheerless thing into this quickly passing world—and wanted to go away, for three months (three would be enough, if she really tried, and worked hard), to learn about talking and feelings and relationships, and come back, then, confident as a friend, real and laughing as a daughter.

"I won," said Chelsea's dad, and went to give Chelsea a high-five, but missed, as they were standing too close.

"My fault," he said. "That was my fault."

"Oh," Chelsea said.

And he stepped back a little and tried again, but Chelsea, distracted now by something—maybe the plant in the far corner, standing and waiting like a person in a dream, or maybe the green shoe or some other thing that was out there and longing, to be looked at, and taken—wasn't ready, and their hands, his then hers, passed through the air in a kind of wave, a little goodbye.